THE TRUTH

KAREN WOODS

THE TRUTH

KAREN WOODS

HarperNorth
Windmill Green,
Mount Street,
Manchester, M2 3NX

A division of
HarperCollins*Publishers*
1 London Bridge Street
London SE1 9GF

www.harpercollins.co.uk

HarperCollins*Publishers*
Macken House,
39/40 Mayor Street Upper,
Dublin 1
D01 C9W8

First published by HarperNorth in 2024

1 3 5 7 9 10 8 6 4 2

A catalogue record for this book
is available from the British Library

ISBN: 978-0-00-859213-4

Printed and bound in Great Britain by
CPI Group (UK) Ltd, Croydon

To my dearest mother Margaret,
I miss you every single day but I know you are looking
down on me and guiding me to where I should be.
To my brother Daz, the years have passed but
I'll never forget you or the fun we had together.
Keep shining bright our kid and watch this space.
To my son Dale, goodnight God bless,
love you always x

Also by Karen Woods

Tracks

Tease

Vice

The Deal

The Con

Chapter One

Yellow light seeped under the bedroom door and lit up the old woman's face – deep wrinkles, dark circles underneath her eyes. The sweet smell of lavender lingered in the air, calming and peaceful. You could tell this woman had been a beauty in her day, but her bright blue eyes now filled with pain no medication could disguise. Brenda Smith's gaze was focused somewhere far away. The windows of the soul, they called them, and, looking deep into her eyes, you could see she was suffering. Her chest rattled with every breath she took – slow, shallow lungfuls. But there was more than physical pain here. Brenda swallowed slowly and turned her head to look at the old silver-framed photo of her three children: Emily, Teresa, and Shannon. A single tear ran down her face and settled on her thin red lips. Her babies, her girls. Brenda's hand trembled as she picked the photo up, stared at the three girls and ran her skinny finger over the image. She whispered, "I'm so sorry, girls. Sorry I let all these years go by and never got in touch. Sorry for everything I put you through. I've prayed every night to the Lord God Above to send you home to me and I hope he's heard my prayers. I want to see the women you've grown up to be. I need to explain, tell you the full truth, tell you all how much I love you."

The light from outside the room suddenly flooded into the bedroom as the door creaked open. Brenda shot a look over to the doorway, but it was only her husband standing there, and she quickly wiped her eyes. If he saw she'd been crying again, he would only tell her to stop worrying about things she couldn't change. But she *could* change it, change it all, make it all right. Sam walked over to her holding a cup of tea and a small yellow fairy cake. She'd always had a sweet tooth and these days cakes were the only thing she enjoyed eating. He placed the plate on the small bedside cabinet next to her and sat on the edge of the bed. He looked drained, the worries of the world on his shoulders. He swallowed hard before he spoke, holding back the tears, trying his best to curb his emotions.

Be strong, man, he told himself. "Come on, Bren, I've brought you a nice little cake and a cuppa. Do you need me to help sit you up?"

Brenda glanced over to the photo again and pointed to her girls. "They're not coming, are they? You've sent them all letters and tried ringing them, but still nothing. They will never forgive me, Sam, not even when they know my time on this Earth will be over soon. I should have told them the truth, helped them understand what I was going through."

Sam gulped, the prospect of losing his wife stabbing deep into his heart, the thought of her not being by his side anymore landing on him like a tonne of bricks. They had been together since he was twenty years old. It had been love at first sight. She was his soul mate, he told everyone. And looking at the two of them together, you could still see love in their eyes. But now she was leaving him and there was not a single thing he could do to change that. He'd fought with the doctors for months, begging them to find a cure for the lung cancer, telling them he would pay for the best treatment money could buy. But the disease was never going to leave her body. Every day it was taking a piece of his wife away from him and not even all the money in the world could stop this cruel condition. He looked deep into her eyes. What would he do without her? How would he cope without her by his side? Was there even a life for him when she was gone? He couldn't see it. Sam's eyes flooded with tears as the ball of emotion rose in his throat, trying to burst through. He closed his eyes and took deep breaths, hoping the tears would subside. He reached over, kissed his wife's slim fingers and dropped his head low.

"They'll come, Bren. Just give them time."

Brenda squeezed his hand tightly and inhaled raggedly as she tried to catch her breath. "That's the one thing I've not got. Sam, I need to tell you this: you have been my source of happiness throughout my life. You picked me up when I was down, and you were always there when I needed you. Even when I didn't deserve it. When I'm gone –" she choked up and looked away from him before she continued: "I want you to be strong, do you hear me? Don't cry for me, because I'll never be far from your side. I'll only ever be a whisper away. I thank you from the bottom of my heart for loving me the way you have over our years together. I know it's not always been plain sailing, but you have always been the man I love with all my heart. You are my happy-ever-after."

Sam snivelled and his shoulders started shaking. His head bowed, emotions crippling him. He licked his cracked lips and kissed her fingertips again. He had to tell her he was weak. He must open up and tell her he wasn't as strong as she thought. "Bren, I'm scared. A life without you is not worth living. You have always been the one I want. How can I go on when I know you won't be here? I've tried to imagine it, tried to find a way that might help, but I can't. I'll never find a way."

She stopped him dead in his tracks, aware he was on the brink of a panic attack. "And that's why I need the girls. Not only to make my peace, but you need them home to help you through this. It's my fault they never came, my fault we haven't seen them for years. And I want to right the wrongs I have done before I leave this Earth. Once I've spoken with them, they will understand, surely."

Sam lifted his head and looked directly into her eyes, the memory of what she did dancing about in his mind. The eyes he looked on now were the same that had lied to him all those years ago; the same eyes that cried and cried when she realised she'd made a mistake. He shook the vision from his mind. The past was the past, and he was far from squeaky clean himself. He never, ever, wanted to feel like that again, never wanted to remember those days. "Come on, love, drink your drink, and try and eat something. Your medication needs to be taken with food and not on an empty stomach. You'll be sick if you don't eat." Sam reached for the plate and broke a small piece from the sticky cake. He placed it in her mouth, smiling as he fed her. "You've always liked sweet things, haven't you, Bren? Chocolate, toffees? And you've been the sweetest thing in my life."

Brenda started to have a coughing fit and he jumped up from the bed to sit her up. Bright blood sprayed from her mouth and her eyes widened with fear. She knew the time to meet her maker would arrive soon, but she was fighting to stay, fighting, with every breath she had left in her body, to see her girls one last time.

Chapter Two

Shannon lay in bed, staring at the black mould creeping across the ceiling like a spider's web. A shit tip, this house was, and the local council had told her they would come by the end of the month to do all the repairs, but so far they'd never been near. A waste of space, they were, utter bobbins. She looked around the bedroom, depressed by her surroundings. Who could call this a home? The window frames were old. Every wall had cracks in it, just like the relationships inside the house, she supposed. Paddy McNulty lay next to her, and she was scared of moving a muscle in case she woke him. He was like a bear with a sore head when he was disturbed – shouting, demanding she look after him. It had been a late one last night and he'd got heavy with his hands again, punching her, shoving her, calling her names. That was the way it went with Paddy – mental abuse, as well as physical. She should have rung the police on the wanker and had him arrested. She was always arguing with the voice in her head that said, if she left him, she would have nowhere to turn, no one to help her. She knew there were restraining orders, refuges all across Manchester, to help women escape violent relationships – she just didn't know if she could find the courage to do it. She touched the swollen side of her cheek gently, remembering the fury etched across his face as he spat at her, telling her she was worthless, a slag, a dirty whore. While his blows left her with constant pain, she told herself she should have learned not to be hurt by his words, by the mental torture he put her through every day. No matter how she tried to cover it up, it happened all the time. Why did she stay? Shannon asked herself every bloody day and she could never come up with an answer. Maybe his hold on her was too deep-rooted. When she first met Paddy, he had made her laugh, told her how beautiful she was, treated her like a lady when times were good, gave her pills to black out the past when times were bad, helped her to forget her life before him. Yet slowly but surely, his behaviour changed, and, before she knew it she was tied to him and it felt too late to get help. She'd become hooked on the tablets he gave her. Then she'd become hooked on him. He'd been dealing a fair bit when they first met and he liked the way the pills made her – docile, compliant, easy to control. But then he'd stopped taking her out with him and, if she was locked up at home, what did it matter if she was high or not? She wished she'd saved some of the stronger pills – they were better than any of the lightweight stuff from the GP. But they were long gone – just like any affection between her and Paddy. He'd stopped dealing, as well – too much like hard work – and got by on the odd dodgy job with his mates. Not that she ever saw a penny of anything he earned. He made sure she knew her place – at home, without any chance of ever getting away.

He'd drummed it into her that if she ever left him, he would search the ends of the Earth for her and make sure she never took another breath. Shannon believed him too. He was a headcase, always fighting when he was out in the boozer, always on the hunt for aggro. Shannon had been with Paddy for over ten years now and, to hear her speak, he was the best thing since sliced bread. At least, that's what she told all her friends on the rare occasions she ever got to see them. But they weren't blind, she knew. They'd seen the bruises, the thick lips, her body shaking. They knew she was lying through her front teeth. The only person she was kidding was herself.

He stirred next to her now. She tried to get a handle on her emotions, to not let him see how rattled she was, then turned to look at him. His eyes shot wide open, staring at her. He pushed her with one of his long, hairy legs.

"Go on, make me a brew. And a couple of pieces of toast wouldn't go amiss."

She paused, waiting to see what else was on his list of morning orders. He booted her leg again, a bit harder this time. A reminder of her role in this relationship.

"Are you fucking deaf woman, or what?"

Shannon eased one of her pale legs out of the bed and then the other. She winced at the pain, not wanting to look down at the bruises and bite marks all over her skin. She stood up and found an old grubby white t-shirt to shove on and a pair of shorts. She was all skin and bones, and the clothes hung off her. The years of drug addiction and pill-popping were taking their toll on her body. She growled at him, forgetting he was still hungover and in a foul mood.

"You're lucky I'm making you anything after last night's performance. Go on, tell me it was my fault again, because that's what you usually say. I did fuck all, Paddy, and yet you laid into me again." She pointed at her face, the marks on her body. "You need to stop drinking if it makes you behave like that. I only said I fancied a curry, and you went off on one, calling me a fat cow. You need to see a doctor or something if you can't control yourself. Tapped in the head, you are."

Paddy ragged his fingers through his thick dark hair, her voice drilling his ears, rattling his hangover. "Ssshh, woman. I was only looking after your figure, that's all. You must have said something else to wind me up. You know what you're like when I'm pissed. You always rub me up the wrong way. Go on, say you don't."

She bent her head towards him, dicing with death. "What, and I deserve a belt for that, do I? Look at my lip."

His eyes changed and he looked at her directly, a look that told her to leave him alone, to keep her mouth shut before it was too late. It would take only seconds for him to jump out of bed and grab her, and what then? Battered again. No, she had to be quiet if she knew what was good for her. Shannon left the bedroom with speed, glancing back over her shoulder to check he wasn't following, and headed straight into the bathroom. Closing the door behind her, she locked it and slid the silver bolt across the door with shaking hands. She knew it wouldn't keep him out if he really wanted to get to her, but it was better than nothing. It made her feel safe for a few minutes. She turned to the bathroom mirror and looked at her reflection. She felt appalled as she stroked the lumps on her cheekbone, saw the finger marks on her skin. She stared at herself for a few seconds, and then scooped her long black hair into a ponytail and tied it back. Long gone were the days when, no matter what time she got up, she always looked pretty. Life with Paddy had stolen her looks, stripped them from her like they were his to take. This was his world now, and she was only existing in it with him. No real life whatsoever, a slave. Paddy was a control freak and he never let her out of his sight for long. If he nipped down to the shops, he locked the door behind him. If he went to the pub, he made sure there was no way out of the house for her. He had even screwed the windows down. Of course, he denied it was to keep her locked inside; said it was so criminals couldn't break in. Bullshit, that was, pure lies. Shannon had a few friends she would see when she was out shopping with Paddy but, even then, he would never leave her side, always made sure he could hear any conversation they were having. He was paranoid she was talking about him behind his back – as if she'd ever have the chance now. A bunch of slags, he called her oldest friends. He didn't even know them properly, just said he could smell a slapper a mile off. Shannon was no more than a prisoner, and he was her jailer. She brushed her teeth, then held her head back, inhaling deep breaths. She checked the cabinet for her pill bottle – but knew it was empty. Anxiety crippled her, and her eyes flooded with tears. Her body folded as she practically melted onto the bathroom floor, knees to her chest, a hand covering her mouth so Paddy could not hear her sobbing. A loud voice shouted from across the landing. She froze.

"Shannon, what the hell are you doing in there? A piss doesn't take that long. I told you to get my breakfast sorted."

She sprang to her feet, aware, if she left it any longer, he would burst through the door and deal with her. That was what he called it when he laid into her for no reason: "I'll deal with you, Shannon. Don't make me fucking deal with you, woman."

Her hands trembled as she unlocked the bathroom door. A quick look one way then the other and she headed downstairs. The house was freezing cold. There was only money for beer and weed, and none for electric and gas. He'd told her straight that if they ran out of gas or electric then it was her fault for not managing the house better. So she kept the heating off as much as she could, trying to save money. Goose-pimples appeared on her white skin. She rubbed at her thin arms to try and get warm. The moment she opened the kitchen door, she heard a snuffle and a black Frenchie came running to her side, jumping about, happy to see her, tail wagging. She smiled for the first time that day. She wished she could sneak Little Frank upstairs and cuddle up to him rather than share a bed with Paddy. But the dog was never allowed upstairs. Paddy said her four- legged friend got more attention than he did and there was no way he was having that scruffy mutt on his bed all night long, keeping him awake. He booted the dog at any given chance, shouted at him, threw things at him. Shannon always put herself between Frank and Paddy to protect the little thing. To her, cruelty to animals was the lowest of the low. She bent down and stroked Frank with her flat palm. Her voice was subdued. "Don't look at me with them eyes. I know what you're thinking. And I know you're right. He said it was my fault. Dealt with me again, hasn't he?"

The dog gave her a disappointed look with eyes that told her he knew her pain. Frank was Shannon's best friend. She told him everything, explained in detail how her life had messed up. She even asked him to help her find a way out, find a life without abuse. She flicked the kettle on and started to make him upstairs a coffee. She smirked at his cup, took the same knife she used for the dog food and gave it a good stir round inside.

"That's our secret, Frank, eh?" she chuckled.

She looked in the cupboards and stared. A few slices of bread and the odd stale biscuit was all that was left. It was her benefits day today. Her universal credit would go into her bank, and yet she would have to ask Paddy if they could go shopping and get some food in. 'Payday', he called it. Days he could sit in the boozer and piss the money up the wall. Yes, he'd bung her a few quid out of her own benefit, but only enough to get the bare essentials. She reached up to the shelf and grabbed the bread. Two slices left, only enough for him. She sighed and popped the bread into the toaster, watched the heat rising, rubbing her hands over it, trying to get warm.

"Bleeding hell, how long does it take to make a bit of toast?" He was behind her now, his hand touching the top of her shoulder.

"It's not my fault the toaster is crap. I've told you time and time again we need a new one."

He walked over to the kitchen side, picked up the kettle and poured some more hot water into his cup. Shannon tried not to smile as he took a slurp from the mug.

"We can go shopping in a bit. Get some foundation on your face first, though, cover them marks. You're not walking about with me looking like that. And don't let me hear you telling anyone I've done it. You deserved it, like always, didn't you?"

Shannon stood with her back to him, buttering the toast. She knew from bitter experience to keep her mouth shut. What was the point in arguing with him, anyway? He'd never admit he was in the wrong. The letterbox rattled and, before she could move, he stepped into the hallway. "Postman's getting later every day. I've a good mind to one-bomb him for taking so long. The post should be here at the crack of dawn, not late morning."

She picked up her coffee and plonked down at the kitchen table, staring into the bottom of her cup as if it held all the answers to her problems. Paddy walked back into the kitchen and dropped three letters on the table before he sat down. Two looked like junk, but one had her name on – a white envelope, handwritten. She sat back in her seat and slid her eyes over it. She knew not to touch the mail. Paddy was the man of the house, he'd told her, and he dealt with anything that came through the front door. Shannon watched him eating his toast, slurping his coffee. He reached over to the letter, frowning as he turned the white envelope over in his hand. Slowly, he opened it. Two sheets, neatly folded. Shannon's eyes were wide open, eager for him to tell her who had sent the letter, but she knew not to let him see her curiosity. He read the first page then placed it face down on the table so she couldn't see the words written there. When the second page was finished, he slammed it down on top of the other one. "A load of shit. Nothing to get excited about."

Shannon played with her fingers, nervously looking over at him. "Who's it from?"

Paddy sparked up a cigarette. He studied her, cunningly. "It's from your old man. Your mam is sick, and she wants to see you."

Shannon sat up straight. "Can I have a read?"

"What for? I've fucking told you what it said. A cheeky bastard, he is, in my eyes. You've not heard a word from him in years and, just because your mam is ill, he wants us to run around after him. No, he can fuck off. Probably trying to get you over there to skivvy for him. Sod that. You've got enough to do looking after this place. What do you say, babes?"

She swallowed hard, knowing she had to agree with him. Her head bowed. "Yep, you're right. It's her fault we lost touch and, like you said, now she's ill she wants me back home. Too much time has passed. I love my dad, but he made his choice, didn't he?"

Paddy sucked hard on his fag and nodded slowly, watching her every movement from the corner of his eye. "Devious sods, they are. They never give a shit about you for all these years. It's me who's looked after you, not them, and now they expect you to go running home because that old hag is on her last legs. Are they having a laugh, or what?"

Shannon never took her eyes from the letter, desperate to read it herself, to make up her own mind. But she knew, if she so much as reached for it, he would have the house up. No, she had to play this cool, not show any interest in the letter. Poker face. She stood up and stretched her arms over her head. "Right, I better get this show on the road and get ready. Are we going shopping? It's payday and we need to go to Asda to get some food in. The cupboards are empty, and we have nowt in the fridge, either."

"Relax, woman, don't be mapping my day out for me when I've only just opened my bleeding eyes. Let me wake up and I'll tell you what we are doing. You don't tell me."

Shannon picked up his empty plate and cup and walked to the kitchen sink. She ran some water and washed the few pots. He was still there behind her, she could feel it. Shannon turned the radio on and started humming. She heard the chair scrape back behind her and flinched as she stirred the hot water. Was he gone or was he still lurking? Sometimes even turning round and looking at him the wrong way was enough to set him off. After a few seconds, she sprayed the dish cloth with the cleaner and started wiping the sides, not sure if he was still in the room. Slowly, she twisted around, looking one way then another. He was gone. She was alone. She rushed to the table and picked up the letter with shaking hands, her heart beating inside her ribcage like a speeding train. She tried to focus on every word her father had written. Time wasn't on her side, and she had to be quick. She gulped as she finished reading the letter. She replaced it carefully where she had found it and rushed back to the kitchen sink. Her bottom lip trembled as her eyes clouded over.

His loud voice behind her made her jump. "Get ready, then. You can finish cleaning when you come back. I'll go shopping with you, then, if you don't mind, I'll have a few hours down the pub with the lads. Hair of the dog definitely needed. I'm going to have a bet and see if I can win us some money. You're OK with that, aren't you?"

She looked out of the window and replied as if he was actually giving her an option. She never had a choice, and he knew it. "Yes, that's fine. I'm going to clean all the windows today, anyway. I can't see out of them anymore. Mucky, they are."

He was still at the doorway – she could hear his heavy breathing behind her. Slowly, she turned around, and he eyeballed her, then the letter. "I'll get rid of this shit, then, should I? I don't want it ruining our day."

She remained calm and kept her eyes on him. "Yeah, do whatever with it. Means nothing to me."

He snatched the bunch of letters from the table. "Go and get ready, then. I'll put these in the bin."

She walked past him and headed upstairs, her cheeks bright red, avoiding eye contact. She'd never been a good liar and even now she struggled to hide the truth.

She sat on the edge of the bed and slipped her black pumps on. They were old now and ready for the bin. In fact, all her clothes were tired and old, but there was never enough money for food, let alone clothes. Every now and then, she would get a new top from the charity shop, but she never told Paddy about it, hid it away in her wardrobe and pretended she'd had it for ages when he asked her where it was from. She'd often nip into the charity shops when he was in the bookie's putting a bet on. He would have gone ape if he thought she was dressing herself up for another man. He would have ripped up any new clothes he found. Paddy knew everything that she owned, everything about her, knew her every move, knew what time she would take a bath each night, knew what she ate and at what time. She quickly brushed her hair and walked over to the bedside cabinet. The bottle of body spray was nearly all gone now, coconut fragrance, a sweet smell. She squirted it over her clothes. After the second spray, she looked at the bottle in more detail. Nope, she wasn't getting any more from it. It had seen its day. She didn't know when she'd have enough money again to get another. She looked into the single mirror on her wardrobe door. She had no shape anymore, no bum, no cheeks, limp hair. Where had it all gone wrong? He was shouting her name now. She'd taken longer than she normally did to get ready. His voice made the hairs on the back of her neck stand on end; her heart missed a beat. "I'm coming. Hold your bloody horses, will you?" she shouted back.

With each step she took down the stairs, his eyes burned into her, checking what she was wearing, checking she had not put any effort into her hair today, nothing to draw attention to herself. "Ready when you are," she said in a sarcastic tone.

Paddy opened the front door and zipped his coat up as the strong northerly wind circled his face. Leaves flew about as if they were performing a dance routine. He walked to the bin and lifted the blue lid up. He shoved the letters out of his jacket down the side of the bin and quickly closed the lid. "Come on, then. And don't think I'm spending all bastard day at Asda. In and out, we are – the lads are waiting for me. I know what you're like once you get in there, looking at all the stuff."

Shannon shut the door behind her and plodded down the path behind him. She wished she had a warmer coat. It was icy cold out – freeze the balls from a brass monkey, it would. But maybe there was something else that could warm her. Shannon shot a quick look behind her at the bin. A letter from her dad, a message that he still loved her. Words that told her someone did care about her after all.

Chapter Three

Emily Rowan sat across the desk, looking at John Spencer, an ex-con who had served five years behind bars. He looked tough, after all, he'd had a hard life, but there was something else in his eyes. He'd been released from the big house six months ago and Emily knew this latest stretch had broken his back, though he'd never admit it. The dodgy food, next to no contact with friends or family, nothing much to do all day but stare at four walls – it took a certain mindset to keep coping with spells inside. Even being released didn't sort everything. Coming out of jail was daunting for most cons, and by the time they arrived in front of her, their heads were usually all over the show, adjusting to life on the outside. Emily had been allocated as John's probation officer from the start and, while on paper he seemed to be adapting to life on the outside, she could tell there was something else going on. Circumstances didn't help – he'd told her he was skint, and she knew more than anyone that poverty could drive a person to make the wrong choices. Maybe that sense of understanding from her own childhood experiences explained why, from the moment Emily met John, she'd felt a connection, a giddiness inside her. She'd had countless similar cases before John, though, so why did she feel like this when he walked into the room? He was a good-looking guy, true, but not someone she would usually be attracted to – younger than her, too. He was a rough and ready type. Emily could feel his eyes all over her as she nervously straightened his paperwork. What the hell was he gawping at?

John sat back in his chair and stretched his hands over his head, cocky and clearly picking up on her discomfort. She couldn't help but look at the strip of brown tanned skin where his t-shirt had risen up. Heat rose to her chest. She was flustered. She swallowed hard, tried to remain professional. "So, John, how have you been? Have you found any work yet?"

He smiled at her and sucked on his teeth before he replied. "Nah, no job as of yet. But who's going to give me a job when I've just got out of the chokey. I'm an armed robber, for crying out loud. No employer will give me the time of the day, love."

She opened her eyes wide as she replied. "And that's why I am asking you: so I can help. We have quite a few employers who do take on ex-cons, often working in warehouses, labouring on building sites. Is that something you would be interested in?"

He hunched his shoulders and rolled his eyes. She could practically read his thoughts: shit wages, doing all the donkey work for next to nothing. But he clearly knew he had to play the game. "Maybe, depends on the pay. I'm not working for peanuts, sack that. I would need a decent wage. The money I get at the moment each week is crap, barely enough to live on. The government need to sort their nappers out and try living on the money we get and see what it feels like. Fuck all, it is. Pennies."

Emily rolled her blue biro around in her fingers and raised her eyebrows. She'd worked as a probation officer for over fifteen years now and, while some of the men she saw were determined to go straight, some of the ex-prisoners she had on her books were bone idle, wanted everything served to them on a plate. She used her schoolteacher voice. "Getting a job would be a great start to changing your life, John. It will give you independence, keep you busy and help you stop re-offending. Looking at your record, there is a pattern of activity after you've been released from jail. You can't let this happen again. You're forty years of age now and it looks like you have spent most of your life in and out of jail. You were in a young offenders' institution when you were seventeen, is that right? That's more than half your life you've been in and out of these places."

John sat cracking his knuckles. Under the spotlight, he was. He hesitated, stuttered, not sure what to say. "Yeah, that's true, but it doesn't tell you in my files the reason why I ended up there, does it? You lot think you know it all, but in reality you know fuck all about the real world. You've probably been fed with a silver spoon, had everything given to you on a plate."

Emily could see he was getting agitated and spoke in a softer tone, the one she used on her own daughter when she was explaining something she didn't understand – or didn't want to hear. "So, tell me. Maybe speaking about things will clear your head. I know I feel better when I talk about things that are getting me down. I'm here to help. You're forgetting that."

John bowed his head and closed his eyes slowly. He sat playing with his fingers. "My mam was a junkie, a raging baghead, if I'm telling it like it is. For years, me and our kid were left to fend for ourselves. No food in our cupboards, no clean clothes. In fact we only had a couple of t-shirts and pairs of keks to our name. Scruffy bastards, we were. Mucky faces all the time. All the kids on the estate called us names." He bit down hard on his lips, then continued: "She left us for days on our jacks. Told us she'd be home later to sort our tea out, and never came back. The bitch. I had two choices back then: break the law, or report my mam to social services."

Emily swallowed hard, grabbed some tissues and passed them over to John: he was getting upset. She sat watching him, eager for him to continue. She guessed he didn't have many chances to be this open. He didn't look like someone who 'did' vulnerable.

"I used to look at my mates with their families, a mam, a dad, and all that. The way they were dressed, how their mothers treated them. I wanted that. Not a big ask, was it? Me and our kid had none of that. We would sit and watch our mam off her rocker most nights, men in her bed who she barely knew. It was hard to grow up around it all. Fucked my head up. Nobody knows the half of it."

Emily nodded. "I bet it was, John. I'm so sorry to hear that." She sat in silence, encouraging him to continue. This was progress. He'd opened up to her, told her how he felt, spoke about the reasons he chose a life of crime. And he was right: none of this was recorded in his file. He was down as a serial offender – not as a survivor of neglect and abuse.

"It started with a bit of shoplifting, mainly food. I was good at it, too. Our Jerry started to come with me and between us we got all we needed not to starve. We hid the food under our beds, never let anyone know what we were doing. I mean," he chuckled. "It's not like my mam would have been arsed, anyway. She would have encouraged us and probably sold the food we nicked to fund her habit."

Emily took a small sip of her cold water. The story was getting to her. We were all just a whisper away from a different kind of life, she thought.

"Anyway, that's where it all started and, before I knew it, I was blazing weed and other drugs and in with a crowd who showed me how to earn the big money." His eyes were wide, his palms sweating. "I was fearless, back then. The first time I was on a graft, I held no fear of what lay ahead. I genuinely had nothing to lose – that's what makes you properly dangerous. I wanted to earn some big money, money that would put my mam in rehab, money that would fill our fridge and buy us some new clobber. I would have risked it all to fix us as a family." His eyes clouded over again, and he swallowed hard as he looked Emily directly in her eyes. "I got enough money for my mam to go into rehab and, the day before she was due to go in, she overdosed on smack. Heartbreaking, that, isn't it? Sad that her life had amounted to nothing. I thought back then that I could save her, make her well again, let her see what her life could be like without drugs. And she was happy, you know, happy she was going in rehab to sort herself out. But she just had to have that one last hit. Drugs ruled her life and, in the end, that was all she really cared about. She was a prisoner to drugs. Heroin took my mother away from me and left an empty shell of a woman who I barely knew anymore. I can't even say I can remember any good times when I was growing up. That's why I blazed the weed, took the drugs myself, to block it all out. But eh, life's a bitch sometimes, isn't it?"

Emily was lost in this man's story. How sad life could be for some people. Without thinking, she reached across and touched his hand. It just happened. She wasn't a robot, and she was showing she cared. "You're a brave man, John. A very brave man indeed. Do you think counselling might help?"

He must have realised now that he'd let his guard down, showed his vulnerable side. He sniffed and sat up straight in his chair. "Nah, fuck all that. I'm alright. Sound as a pound, I am. I'm not spending hours talking about shit I can't change. Pointless."

Emily smiled gently. Her heart melted for this man; he'd had to do what he'd done to help his little brother and try to save his family. He was right: he had done what he had to do, taken the only options available. Maybe someone should have asked him about his past, delved deeper and got to the bottom of his criminal activity before it was too late. That first time in the nick could have been his only stint if they'd helped him then. Same old story though, wasn't it; the government never had enough money to treat people who had mental health issues. They simply fell under the radar. Easier to bang someone up than to fix them. Emily sighed; God knew she understood how it felt to have problems in her life. Her family was dysfunctional too and, although she hid behind the perfect life now, she had her own skeletons in her cupboard, just like everybody else did. She coughed to clear her throat and carried on with the session.

"I can give you some phone numbers if you want a list of employers we work with?"

John gave a cheeky smile and winked at her. "I'd rather have *your* phone number."

Emily felt herself go bright red, cheeks burning. She stuttered, panicked. "I'm afraid I'm a married woman, John."

"Makes no difference to me. If I'm being honest about everything, I've had a thing for you since our first meeting. Swear to God, I look forward to my appointments just to spend some time with you."

Emily self-consciously flicked her hair back over her shoulder and stared at him. A wave of heat surged through her body from her feet to the back of her neck. She felt weak at the knees. John was good-looking in his own way, and she hated to admit it, but she too had had a soft spot for him since the moment she met him. But what was she thinking? She needed to give her head a shake. She was strictly forbidden from getting too close to service-users. She smiled awkwardly and repeated her words, trying to ignore their hollow ring. "Like I said, I'm married, John. But, even if I weren't, I'm not allowed to date my clients."

He laughed out loud and sat forward in his seat. "Can I say something without you reporting me?"

Emily should have put an end to the conversation right there and then, but she was intrigued at what he was going to say next. What harm could it do? She checked her watch and shot him a look. "Yes, but make it quick, because our session is due to end."

"If things were different, and there wasn't this desk between us, I would love to make love to you, to kiss every inch of your body. I've imagined it so many times, and I know you would enjoy it."

Emily flushed scarlet and looked down at her notes to hide her face. Bleeding hell, she was fifty-five years of age, and she was blushing like a teenager. Why on Earth was he interested in her? She couldn't bring herself to reply to his comment, deciding it was safest to ignore it and let the moment pass. She stood up and gathered her paperwork together. "Right, I'll see you again next week. If you change your mind about employment, then let me know."

But he was standing next to her now and looking directly into her eyes. His warm breath made the skin on the side of her neck prickle. "And, if you change *your* mind, just let me know." As he walked past her, his body nearly brushed against hers and she could feel an almost magnetic pull. "See you next week, lovely," he said as he left the room.

Emily stood with her back against the wall and had to take a few minutes to regain her composure. Her heart was racing, and she was in a panic. No one had spoken like that to her for years, and she hadn't realised how much she'd missed the feeling of being desired. Truth be told, for one mad moment, she could have ripped his clothes off right there and then and fulfilled his every need. Her home life was crap at the present, and sex was a distant memory. The only action she had with her husband was a quick shag before *Corrie* or on his birthday or a special occasion. She often asked herself if it was her fault or his, and she could never make her mind up. Maybe, they were just too old now, took each other for granted. Or maybe she had never forgiven him. You forgive, but you don't forget. Emily looked down at John's file and went through his list of convictions. He was dodgy, for sure, a con man, someone who would have your eyes out and come back for the sockets. He was everything she'd spent her life avoiding. Why then, had his words lit a fire in her?

Later that evening Emily sat at the dining table and looked over at her husband, Archie. She'd been married to him for over thirty years now and, although they'd had their ups and downs, they were still everyone's idea of a solid couple.

Archie raised his eyebrows. "Whoops, I forgot to tell you, a letter came for you today." He stood up and walked over to the sideboard. He gave the white envelope to his wife just as their daughter, Jena, came to join them at the table. Emily placed the letter on the table beside her, and said to Jen, "I'm glad you're here. I've seen a few jobs advertised that you might be interested in?"

"Mam, I've told you before, I'll find a job when I'm good and ready. Wow, every time I see you lately, all you do is moan. Let me do my own thing. I earn money doing bits of jobs for my friends, like cleaning and ironing for them, so back off." Jena grabbed a piece of bread and started to make a chip butty.

Her dad rolled his eyes and shook his head. "Why do you eat like you've never been fed? Bleeding hell, watch your fingers – you nearly bit them off."

Jena smiled and carried on eating her tea. Emily looked at the envelope next to her, then picked it up and opened it. As she started to read it, her jaw dropped. She finished reading and placed the letter on her lap.

"Are you alright, love? "Archie asked.

Jena was alert, too. "Mam, you look like you've seen a ghost. Who's the letter from? Are you OK?"

Emily quickly filled her glass with the red wine from the table and gulped a large mouthful. Archie was getting impatient. "So, are you going to tell me?"

Jena stared at her mother, waiting on her reply.

"It's from my dad. My mam is ill, and she wants to see us all."

Archie furrowed his brow. "Do what you deem fit, love. But I'll say this, it's been a lot of years and you only get one mother, don't you? Maybe go and see her, and let bygones be bygones."

Emily was in a panic by now. She stood up and started to walk around the room, her glass of wine held firmly in her hand. "What, go and see her after all this time? Why has it taken her to be ill to want to see us all? She should have been knocking at my door when a week had passed after it all happened, but no, she stayed hidden away and let my dad do her dirty work. She could have written me a letter every day telling me how she felt, because, if that was Jena, I wouldn't stop until we were friends again."

Jena chirped in and started laughing out loud. "And don't I know it. We only fall out for ten minutes and you're banging on my bedroom door, wanting to speak to me."

Emily was talking to herself as she paced around the room. "I wonder if he's contacted the others. Our Teresa will collapse if she gets a letter. I know we're not that close, but we still have a sisterly bond. OK, maybe not with Shannon, but come on, the last time we saw her she was off her napper waffling on about the guy she was seeing."

Archie swallowed hard and sat up straight in his chair, avoiding eye contact. "It's been years, Emily. Too many bloody years have passed without it getting sorted. This should have been put to bed ages ago. Family feuds are not good. Look at Jena: she's the one who's missed out on your mam and dad, and her aunties, too. I can count on one hand how many times you've seen your sisters in the last twenty years."

Jena agreed. "He's right, Mam. Your side of the family is messed up. I've missed out on all sorts because of this feud you have going on. Hold on, I tell a lie: I get a birthday card from Shannon every year, but that's about it.

Teresa doesn't even bother sending me a card. And I don't think I'd recognise my grandparents if they knocked on my own front door."

Emily sat back down at the table and ran a finger around the edge of her glass. The colour had drained from her cheeks and her skin looked grey. "I'll ring Teresa later and see if she's had a letter. If I can that is; I'm not even sure if Teresa is on the same phone number. She changes that like she changes her men. There's no point in trying to contact Shannon, though, I know that much. God knows we tried. The last number I had for her doesn't work. And the last time we spoke she asked me not to ring her and said she would ring me. Something to do with the guy she's with, apparently: he doesn't like her getting phone calls. You're right she still sends a birthday card, but she never gets in touch to say she's got the ones we send."

Jena said, "Shannon is an idiot. I've not heard much recently but a couple of years back I was always hearing chat about her from people who'd seen her pilled up. She always gets with men who are dodgy from what you say. You said you've never known her to have a decent bloke who treats her right. That's why she's always taking those tablets, I bet. She must be messed up in the head."

"Oi, you. That's still my sister. And yes, you might be right, but she's been through a lot and, if that's how she copes, then that's how she copes. She's never been strong-willed. Our Teresa is the one with the balls in our family. Me and Shannon were always the people-pleasers. Anything for an easy life."

Archie butted in, "So, try Teresa and, if you get through, ask her to come back home to Manchester and sort this mess out. I bet the three of you got the same letter, so sit down like adults and come up with a solution. I know you would just go with the flow, Emily, but, like you said, Teresa is the one who calls the shots."

Emily's back was up now, and she slammed her flat palm onto the dining table, causing the plates to shake. "Archie, I have a mind of my own. Nobody tells me what to do anymore. Maybe when we were all younger Teresa might have decided everything, but not now. I'm my own person, and if I decide that I want to go and see my mam and dad then that's what I'll do – with or without my sisters. So put that in your pipe and smoke it."

Jena was shocked and covered her mouth with one hand as she looked over at her dad, waiting on his reply.

"Calm down, will you? I'm not saying you are a follower. I'm just saying that, in the past, Teresa has been the one who says what's what. If I've upset you, then I'm sorry. I'm only trying to help. Bleeding hell, shoot me for even caring." Archie blew a laboured breath and carried on eating. He couldn't do right for doing wrong, these days.

Chapter Four

Teresa looked over at the older man sat facing her and smiled. He was her meal ticket tonight. She sipped her drink and licked her lips slowly, gazing into his small beady eyes. "The bubbles from this champagne are making me feel giddy," she purred.

The man kept his voice low, double-checking around him that no one could hear. "I would like to go back to the hotel room now, if that's alright with you. I think the tablet I've taken for my old fella is kicking in. We have to be quick before it wears off. I only usually get an hour or so out of it."

This was music to her ears – the quicker this was over the better. She stood up and reached for her navy-blue Chanel clutch. "Ready when you are, Teddy."

The old geezer scraped his chair back and made his way to the lift with a wobble. There was no way he was taking the stairs. He needed to keep all his energy for the bedroom. Teresa checked herself in the mirror as they waited. Slim figure, pearly white teeth and shoulder-length red hair – she had to look after her assets in her line of work.

Upstairs, Teddy lay on the bed in his silk boxer shorts. He knew the script, had been with brasses all his life. His eyes never moved from her as she started to get undressed, giving him an eyeful before the main event. "I want to see everything, love. Tease me. Keep this old fella ready for action."

Teresa watched as he gripped his crotch. If she played her cards right, this trick would be over in minutes. As requested, she continued to strip, her body bending slowly and suggestively with every movement. Teddy was like a dog on a hot day, almost panting with anticipation. Just as she thought she might have overdone it, she timed the question. It was a tactic she'd honed through the years: show them just enough of what they were in for, then get the money upfront. 'No pay, no play' was her golden rule now. At the beginning, she'd been had over– dodgy guys having sex with her and not paying the rate they'd agreed. More than once, a punter had their way then told her to "Fuck off," said she was a dirty scrubber and she wasn't getting a carrot. But those days were long gone.

"Teddy," she purred, her long black eyelashes fluttering. "Can we sort out the money first? I hate asking for it, but you know as well as me that this is a business deal, and before I deliver the goods I need the money tucked away safely. You can always give me a nice tip and I can do that little thing you like." She gave him a cheeky wink and he blushed. Kinky old git, he was. Always wanted stuff his wife would never give him. After all, Teddy

Mason had been a client of Teresa's for over a year now. Every Monday night, while his wife was at the Women's Guild, he would tell her he was nipping back to the office and come to this hotel and pay for his guilty pleasures. He was a sweet enough old man and she felt safe with him, which was more than she could say about some of the guys she used to see. Nothing much surprised her now, and she'd heard every reason in the book for visiting an escort. Some guys were lonely, but lots had partners – some were ill, working away, or simply didn't like sex anymore. Other guys had things they wanted to do that they were too shy to ask their wives for. Other clients simply wanted some kindness. She wondered if Teddy was one of those. He'd spoken about his wife a little over the time they had spent together, and he'd always told her she was a crank, a power freak who loved to control him. Maybe he was suffering from domestic violence behind closed doors, because some of the stories he'd told her about his other half made her toes curl. But then again, just as she'd learned not to judge any of her customers, she'd also learned not to take their sob-stories at face value. Some of them couldn't manage two honest words in a row. As long as the cash was there, though, Teresa didn't care.

Teddy fanned out two hundred pounds on the end of the bed and quickly shoved his black leather wallet back into his neatly folded navy trousers on the chair next to him.

"No tip then, Ted," she chuckled as she counted the money.

The old man went bright red and licked his thin lips. "Sorry, love, not tonight. I've only drawn out two hundred pounds. If you want, you can give me a treat and I'll settle with you next time."

Teresa stashed the money in her bag and shoved it under the dressing table. It was time now to get this show on the road and get it over with. Back in her day, she earned good money every night, had lots of cash to enjoy the finer things in life – handbags, perfumes, even exotic holidays. But she was younger then, fitter, a woman every man wanted on his arm. She was still a looker, but these days she got more trade by playing the cheeky wife rather than the innocent young woman. And she didn't have the energy to be out every night. She liked her own bed – alone – too much. She wasn't risking her neck fighting the new younger girls for business, so she just worked when she could. But it meant times were harder than they used to be.

She checked the time on her wristwatch. The debt collectors would be knocking at her door soon, booming it down, screaming her name at the tops of their voices. She was in debt up to her eyeballs and with every bit of money she earned she was paying these heavies off. It was her lavish lifestyle that had got her into debt. She'd always thought she would earn big again and be able to pay this money off. She hadn't saved a penny from her glory days. And, when her looks started to fade, her client list got shorter and the money was nowhere near what it used to be. If she looked back ten years ago, she'd been on yachts, the Caribbean sunning her body, with some rich guy.

She'd never wanted for anything. But she'd escaped worse things than this, so she told herself she could do it again. Something had to give. She had to find a way out of this dark hole she'd fallen into. Debt was a prison sentence, and she wanted out.

Teddy was ready now, she could tell. Any longer and the old codger would explode. She had to be quick, give him what he wanted. She kept her black high-heeled shoes on, stepped onto the bed and straddled him. He always wanted her to leave the shoes on. Turned him on, he said. She was astride him now and she could tell – a few moments and he'd be done. Teddy groaned and his toes curled as he grunted a couple of times. He was done. Bleeding hell, that was quick – even for him. Teresa smiled and ran her long talons over his pot belly, playing with the few grey hairs scattered there. She flicked her hair back, then leaned forwards and kissed his hot cheeks. "That was amazing, Teddy. You're my best lover."

Her client went bright red. He was struggling to breathe, and he wanted her off his chest. Teresa lay at his side and pretended to scroll through her phone while Teddy calmed down. Craftily, she positioned the mobile phone above her head. She did it so quickly, Teddy wasn't aware she was even taking photographs, let alone that they were of him. She had made sure she had everything she needed to get a good few quid out of this old boy if she needed to. She'd always had to get insurance the unconventional way. And these days she needed it more than ever.

Messages were constantly coming through on her phone, demands for money from the people she owed.

Maybe it was time to leave the area and start again, start with a clean slate. It would be nice to not always be looking over her shoulder when she walked the streets. This time, she hadn't borrowed money from local lads. Gavin Turner was one of the main men in the north west, and everyone knew he was a force not to be messed with.

Teresa had been seeing Gavin for a few months, sucking him off for money when he was off his head and twisted. That was when she'd asked him for a ten-thousand-pound loan, told him it was to buy a new car, and promised she would give it him back as soon as she was on her feet. But the truth was she never had got back on her feet and, though she was paying him back in dribs and drabs, a couple of hundred here and a couple of hundred there, she still owed more than she'd ever borrowed. He started asking for payment in kind, and she'd said yes at the start – anything to be able to skip a repayment week. But then he got rougher, getting a kick out of humiliating her, and she started making excuses. At first, he didn't seem to mind, but as the months passed and she wasn't opening her door to him and giving him sex for free, the terms got worse. Already he'd booted her front door in and battered her, getting nose-to-nose with her, telling her he wanted his money back in full. She knew he was running out of patience, and she needed to do something quick.

Teresa looked at Teddy. He was loaded – could easily afford to help her. And, in her eyes, he shouldn't be doing what he was doing when he was a married man. So, this would have to be his penance; he would pay extra for his guilty pleasure, or she would tell his wife. So many of the men she slept with were desperate to tell her all about their lives, where they worked, how much money they earned, even where they were going on holiday with their family. They loved showing off their status as if to prove to her that their choice to come to a brass wasn't because of something they were missing. What did they expect? That it would never come back to haunt them? Teresa placed her mobile phone on the bedside cabinet and reached her arm across to hug Teddy. "I wish we could run away together, baby. Just me and you in the sunshine, living life to the full. You've said yourself you have feelings for me, and it hurts me deep inside knowing you go back home to your wife after leaving me. I know I am a working girl, but I still have feelings, don't I?"

Teddy rolled onto his side and stroked her face with his chunky fingers. "I wish we could too, love, but I have work, money to earn, family I cannot walk away from."

"So, buy a house for us in the countryside, a holiday home in the sun, and I can wait there for you until you can get away. It will be like we are married, and I will pretend you are working away from home when you're not there with me." Teresa watched his every movement. He could make all her troubles go away, move her to a quaint little cottage in the countryside where nobody knew her past.

"Maybe in the future, pet. At the minute, I'm involved in some great new deals at work, and I'm set to make serious profit, but all my money is tied up for now. You know the game – you've got to invest for success – the biggest risk is taking no risks at all."

Teresa squirmed. A cheeky bastard, he was. She could sniff out a lie a mile off. He wanted to have his cake and eat it, whisper sweet nothings into her ear and never give her a single thought once he'd slept with her and gone home to his wife. Teddy was as bent as a nine-bob note and he'd slipped up a few times telling her about what he'd invested in. She knew it wasn't all above board – he'd funded drug deals, bought knocked off goods. Well, she'd had enough of it. She was sick to death of watching other people pocket the big bucks. She must take the law into her own hands. She needed a way out, and he was her meal ticket. It was his own fault; he should have been faithful to his wife, kept it in his pants. Blackmailing her clients wasn't good practice, but she'd done it before, and she'd do it again to get herself out of this shit, if he wouldn't help her out without the extra persuasion.

She rolled out of bed and clutched her mobile phone close to her body. There were enough photographs stored on here to get a nice few quid out of this old fart. Teddy was getting ready to leave, making sure he looked respectable, no creased clothes, as he left the hotel room. Teresa started to pick up her clothes and then had a thought. "Hey, babes. Can you keep the room on for me tonight? It's late and I'm not looking forward to getting a taxi at this hour."

Teddy nodded. "It's paid for, anyway. I never book a hotel room for a few hours: causes too many questions. Plus, the wife would be all over it. This way, I can tell her it's a business partner who's staying in town. Yes, stay here and have a good sleep."

Teresa put on a look of relief and walked back to the bed. She eyeballed her client and patted the space at the side of her. "You can always stay with me and have some more fun." She raised her eyebrows as she smiled at him. "I could do that thing you've always asked for. Ring the Mrs. Tell her something's turned up and you will see her in the morning. You've done it before, so I don't see it being a problem."

"No, no. I need to go home this time. I've got a big meeting in the morning and need to be fresh, in clean clothes. Maybe next time."

Teresa sank her face into the pillow and bit down hard. If he'd stayed, she could have got more money out of him, charged him for a full night. Teddy put his navy jacket on and walked over to the full- length mirror. He brushed his hand along his trousers and quickly straightened his thick grey hair. He approached the mirror and looked deep into his eyes. Teresa could see guilt, the look he always got after he'd been doing things he shouldn't have been doing. All he wanted to do now was to get out of here, forget about his guilty pleasure, go home and be the perfect husband his wife thought he was. Teresa looked over at him and knew what he was thinking. He was always the same after sex: regrets, telling himself he would never do it again. But he always came back, always rang Teresa to fulfil his deepest desires.

Teresa pulled the duvet over her body and looked out at the night sky, pitch-black with only a sprinkle of stars out tonight. At least she would sleep peacefully here without the worry of her front door being boomed down. But tomorrow was just around the corner and her problems would still be here when she opened her eyes. She had to think fast, get some money together and leave this town forever. There was too much history here, too many reminders of her sordid past and the men she'd bedded. She scrolled through the photographs she'd taken of Teddy and smiled. What was it he'd said? 'The biggest risk is taking no risks at all'? It was time to test that theory. She was going all-in.

Chapter Five

Shannon sat on the sofa and yanked the small grey blanket over her legs. She was freezing. It was extra cold tonight and, even though she'd tried to keep the heating off, she was just too cold. Surely Paddy would let her have a few quid on the meter. Frank lay at her side and snuggled into her, shivering too. He was only allowed on the sofa when Paddy was out and, as soon as she heard him coming in through the front door, Shannon would make sure the dog was on the floor, nowhere near the sofa, definitely nowhere near Paddy. He'd only start ballooning, moaning that the mutt was ruining the furniture. It was old anyway, hardly a precious antique.

Shannon dug deep into her pocket and pulled out the white pieces of paper; the letter was stained and still stank of the bin. She should have left it where it was, but the urge to read it and read it again was strong. These were her father's words, words she'd missed over the years, him talking to her, telling her everything was going to be alright. He could always calm her down, her father could. Whenever she thought there was no way out, he would sit her down and help her find the answers to anything troubling her. She unfolded the letter slowly, listening for signs that Paddy was coming home. It was still early though, and she never expected him home until the late hour. He was probably still kicking off down the boozer, shouting his mouth to some poor old man who'd done nothing wrong to him. He was like that, Paddy: a bully. One evening when he'd allowed her to come to the pub with him, she was made to sit in the corner and keep her head down. She'd watched him getting drunker and drunker, and louder and louder. He thought he was a hard man but, when she'd watched him that night, he was more like the village idiot. But even in that state, he was still looking for trouble. Paddy would stand at the bar and scan the room for anyone who he thought was giving him a funny look. Once he'd found his target, his eyes half closed, he would stagger over to them and flip the table over to get to them. The poor blokes didn't have a clue what they'd done wrong, he just weighed into them until someone stopped him. Shannon often prayed he would get his comeuppance, that someone would jaw him and put him on his arse. But, up to now, her prayers had not been answered. Her big knobhead of a boyfriend was still walking around like he was the dog's bollocks, making her life a misery.

Shannon squeezed her eyelids and pulled the blanket around her as she settled down to read the letter again. Her eyes clouded and a lump rose in her throat as she read the words her father had written again and again. The big question now was how could she get to see him? How could she ever be free from Paddy? He would never ever let her go. He'd told her point-blank he would put her in a body bag if she ever wronged him or showed him up by trying to leave him. She lifted her head slowly and dabbed the corner of the blanket to her eyes to soak up the tears. Maybe she could ring one of her sisters, tell them about the letter, see if they had received one too. But she'd not spoken to either of them in years. To say there was bad blood between them was an understatement. Teresa had said things to her she would never forget, words that rolled about in her mind when she was stressed and feeling low. Yes, she had been a pill-popper, but being called a druggie by her own flesh and blood felt like daggers being stabbed deep into her heart. And Teresa hadn't stopped there, either. She had fired her insults out one after the other, calling her a slag, a pathetic excuse of a woman, a low-life. And maybe she was, but to hear it from her sister was something she could never get her head around. She could have retaliated, given her a mouthful, told her she knew her dirty little secret, but she kept schtum to save the peace. People who live in glass houses, and all that.

Emily was always the voice of reason in the family and, like her dad, she was a problem-solver. Shannon had always gone to her for help when she was younger, but not since she'd ruined all of that. Emily was the good girl of the family – eldest daughter, married first. Shannon doubted Emily would ever really forgive her for what she'd done, despite saying she had. No, as always, she was on her own.

After reading the letter a last time, Shannon stood up, walked over to the corner of the room, yanked the thread-bare carpet up and slid the letter underneath it. She stood on top of it, jumping around to make sure there were no signs that anything was underneath there. Paddy was like *CSI: Manchester*. As soon as he walked into a room he could see if anything had been shifted, even the slightest of movement. She'd only moved the clock a few inches on the television to clean it, and he saw it straight away, asking why she was moving things about. Shannon walked back to the sofa and unscrewed the white lid from a tablet bottle. She emptied a handful of pills into her hand and necked them with a quick drink of water. These were her calmers that made her body melt away and her troubles subside. She'd be asleep in half an hour, dead to the world, and hopefully, when she woke up in the morning, Paddy would no longer be there. With any luck he would have got arrested, put on his arse by someone in the pub, and be lying in a hospital bed being fed through a tube. Frank shifted while she sat back down and, once she was comfortable, he lay across her body. Maybe he knew she was cold. He knew her life better than anyone else did in the whole wide world. Shannon's eyes began to close slowly.

The front door swung open, cold air flying in from outside. Paddy wobbled as he stood at the front door trying to pull his key out from the lock. "Fuck off, the lot of you can go and fuck off. I need nobody but myself," he mumbled as his legs buckled under him. His body crashed into the wall with a loud thud. "Bastards, who is it? Come on, show yourself, you prick, and I'll fight you." Paddy rolled about the floor in a drunken stupor fighting invisible enemies, then pressed his hands against the wall, trying to get to his feet. His size tens booted at the front door to close it. Silence for a few seconds. He lay staring at the ceiling and his nostrils flared as his face filled with anger. He was back on his feet now, holding onto the wall as he staggered into the front room. Frank jumped down from the sofa and hid away under the table. He knew his master's voice and already he was shaking from head to toe. Paddy sucked hard on his gums before he spat across the room. He spotted her now, saw feet hanging from the sofa. He wobbled again. "Yes, you fucking sent them, didn't you? Fucking slag, dirty no-good bitch who brings fuck all to the table. I could have had any woman in that pub tonight. The women were all over me and yet I come home to you fucking moaning and going on. Look at you," his words slurred. "Hanging, you are. Fucking stinking scruffy bitch." He dragged at her feet, ragging them one way then another, white spit hanging from the corner of his mouth. "Wake up, do you hear me? Fucking wake up. Let's sort this shit out once and for all. I might be drunk but I know you are a slut. Where is he hiding? Did he just fuck you and get off? Yeah, I don't blame him. No man in their right mind would stay longer than they needed to with you. Bad news, you are, bad fucking news."

Shannon's eyes shot wide open. She wasn't sure what was happening, her vision blurred. She wriggled and broke free of him, then sat up. Her eyes met his and she knew then she was in serious trouble. His fists curled into two tight balls at his sides and his teeth clenched. He stepped forward slowly, his legs still unsteady. "Where is he? Go on, which way did he go out? Was it through the fucking window?"

She gulped and brought her knees up tightly to her chest. Her voice quivered. "Paddy, go to bed, you're pissed again. Nobody has been here. For crying out loud, you screwed the windows down, so how could anyone get in or bleeding out?"

He screwed his face up and roared at her like a caged lion. "Shut up! For fuck's sake, shut up. Your voice is going through me, woman. Get your stuff together and fuck off out of this house. Go on, get everything you own and leave me to be happy."

Shannon wasn't sure what to do. She hesitated for a few seconds and then stood up and headed towards the living room door. Bad mistake. He was testing her just like he always did.

He gripped her by the hair and swung her around like a rag-doll. "Oh, so you would leave me, would you? I knew there was somebody else. Tell me his name, tell me who it is, and you can have him, you slapper."

Shannon was on the floor, and he pressed his foot onto her chest, restricting any air getting into her lungs. She panicked, words fighting to get out of her mouth. "There is nobody else – take your foot off me – I can't breathe."

He bent down and picked her up by the scruff of the neck. "Does this face look like it gives a fuck?" His head went back and he headbutted her. Then he was pummelling fists into her body, kicking, punching, screaming. Eventually he stood back and looked about the front room. He turned and went into the hallway.

Shannon heard his footsteps going upstairs. Her eyes were only half open, but she spotted the dog under the table. Frank crept out and lay at her side. He curled next to her and never flinched, watching the door. She could feel warm blood trickling down from her nose. She closed her eyes, placed both hands over her mouth and sobbed her heart out. If he heard her crying, he would come down, get back in her face, telling her to cry on the inside like a strong person did, like *he* did when he was hurting. Shannon cringed in pain as she scrambled back onto the sofa. "Bastard," she mumbled under her breath. "Dirty, no-good bastard."

He'd be asleep in no time at all, dead to the world, and maybe this time she could break free, run and run and never look back. But the devil on her shoulder urged her on, said she could creep up the stairs and attack him while he slept, whack the silver claw hammer over his head, break every bone in his bastard body, show him how it felt to be helpless. But right now, she could barely move, let alone launch a counter-attack.

It took all the strength she had just to roll over and reach for her fags. She cursed: there was only a couple left. Her shaking hands held the cigarette tightly as she flicked the lighter. Sucking in, her cheeks sank as she inhaled a long drag. A cloud of thick grey smoke blew from her mouth as she sat watching the living room door. She could hear him upstairs, falling about, talking to himself, fighting whoever he thought was in the room with him. A nutter, he was, a couple of butties short of a picnic. Frank jumped back onto the sofa and placed his warm head on her lap as she wiped the blood on the blanket. His eyes met hers. "Don't look at me like that, Frank. What can I do, eh? I'm sorting it, though. It will just take time, and when I do go you will be coming with me. But let me think about this, get my head together, come up with a plan." She reached for the tablet bottle again and emptied another handful of pills into her hand before she necked them. She sat in the dark and waited for oblivion.

Chapter Six

Emily looked into the silver mirror and shook her hair over her shoulders. She puckered her lips before she applied her peach melba lip-gloss. She'd made an extra bit of effort this morning. She always looked professional, but today she looked a little bit funky, sexy even. She'd taken extra time to make sure she was on point.

Archie walked into the bedroom and clocked her sitting there. "You're late this morning, love. Usually you're having a brew with me at this time."

She stood up and started looking around the bedroom for her shoes. "Yeah, I know. Just thought I would take my time this morning and make an effort. I'm sick of rushing about and, let's face it, I don't get any medals for getting into work early, do I?"

Archie noticed she looked different. "Have you done something to your hair?" He held his head to one side, puzzled. Emily blushed, no eye contact. "Oi," he squawked before she could answer. "Do you know you can see your bra through that white blouse? I'm getting a right eyeful here, let me tell you."

She quickly reached into the wardrobe and grabbed her navy blazer. "I'm wearing my jacket, so nobody will see." She put her jacket on and made sure the button was fastened.

Archie was still looking at her strangely. "I'll make you a drink before you go."

He was gone now, and she was rushing about the bedroom getting everything she needed together for work. Emily stood in front of the mirror and sprayed her perfume all over her body. Looking at her reflection, she smiled and nodded.

Archie wolf-whistled as she came into the kitchen. She blushed again, not used to receiving any kind of compliment on the way she looked. "Oh, piss off, Archie. I've backcombed my hair, that's all. I'm sick of looking the same every day for work. I fancied a change. In fact, I'm going to chuck all my old clothes out and revamp my wardrobe. It's been ages since I bought anything new. Honest to God, my knickers are threadbare, and my bras are a wash away from the bin."

"Do whatever makes you happy, love. I think you look lovely."

Emily sat down at the table and sipped her coffee. She looked up to the ceiling. "Wake Lady Muck up at ten this morning. She asked me last night, but I've got a few meetings booked today and I won't have time to give her a ring."

Archie nodded. "Yeah, I'm in the office all day, so I'll give her a bell. Where is she going, did she say?"

Emily let out a laboured breath. "Did she 'eck. You know what she's like, you only have to ask where she's going and World War Three breaks out. I give up with her, on my life. I'm sick of having the same conversations with her every bleeding day. She's an adult now. She needs to get a job. I've told her we can't keep bailing her out when she's skint. On my life, I've never known anything like it. Both of us are grafters, yet she thinks she can lie in bed and doss all day, without a care in the world."

Archie sat munching his toast and spoke with a gob full. "It's the youth of today, love, no get up and go. It's our own fault for spoiling her. She's never wanted for anything in her life because we've handed it to her on a plate. Every job she's had, she's found something she didn't like about it. I've told her time and time again that nobody likes bleeding working. She thinks she should be laughing all day long, drinking wine, singing. She'll come down to Earth with a big bang one day and realise how important earning a crust is."

Emily took another mouthful of her drink and stood up. "Have you seen my car keys?

"Yes, under the newspaper on the side there. I spotted them last night and knew you would be looking for them. You should put them on the hook there with all the other keys and then you won't ever be looking for them, will you?"

Archie stood up and took his grey jacket from the back of the chair as his wife replied, "We can't all be perfect like you, can we, Archie?" Emily stared at him a lot longer than she should have.

He stuttered, "I'm far from perfect, love. I just like things in order, that's all."

Emily hooked her handbag over her shoulder and swung her car keys around her index finger. "Right, I'm off. Don't forget to ring Jena at ten. I better hurry up before I get caught up in the traffic. See you later. Oh, and shall we get a takeaway for tea tonight? I need to go shopping, and there's nothing in for tea."

"Yeah, no worries. I'll ring for it when you get in so it's nice and fresh. We could be celebrating Jena getting a job, if it all goes to plan."

Walking out of the door, Emily said sarcastically, "Let's not get our hopes up, eh? We both know her of old. She will have some excuse why she's still not employed. She always does. See you later."

Emily sat in her office, and kept looking at the wall clock, edgily. Her diary was open, and she'd circled the name of her next client in thick blue biro. John Spencer would be here in ten minutes. She was nervous, jumpy. She felt she couldn't leave her desk, even to grab a coffee, and instead was merely passing time until he arrived. She checked over her shoulder to make sure her colleague, Nancy Jakes, was nowhere to be seen. Nancy was a proper brown-noser and, at any given chance, she was straight through the line-manager's door, telling her that staff were shopping online instead of working. She was the kind of colleague who'd rather get ahead by criticising others rather than doing any hard work herself. Nancy was twenty years younger than Emily and, to look at her, you would have thought butter wouldn't melt in her mouth, but she was a born snake, always ready to stab daggers in your back when you were not looking. Maybe she didn't have any friends, had been bullied in school or something, because why on Earth would a person do a daily report on her work colleagues when she would get nothing out of it for herself? If she had been one of her clients, Emily would be trying to get to the bottom of her issues. But she wasn't here to give her colleagues therapy. Not that Nancy would stand for being the one in the hotseat. She was happier knowing everyone else's business. A natural busybody. Everybody in the office swerved her like the plague when she was nosing around.

In defiance, Emily clicked onto the Zara website Jena was always talking about. Sombre-looking girls, models who could have done with a pan of stew down their necks to fatten them up. She carried on scrolling through the website regardless, hoping to find something she would suit. But she was struggling – long flared trousers and cropped tops were nothing she would ever look good in: not now, not ever. Finally, she found some tops that would be just right – and might make her feel up-to-date. She saved a lot of blouses to her basket. There was no way she was sitting here going through her bank details and adding her address when Nosey Nancy was on the prowl.

Just as she changed the screen, Nancy came over. "Emily, John Spencer is in reception."

Emily kept her eyes locked on her screen, pretending she was busy. "Thanks, Nancy. Tell him I will be out soon. I just need to finish this report and I'll be ready for him."

Nancy peeped over her shoulder and shot a look at the screen, trying to read what was written there before she marched off.

Emily swallowed hard as she logged off her computer. She picked up John's file and casually flicked invisible dust from her shoulder, taking deep breaths, calming herself down. He was just a man, nothing more, nothing less. She could do this. She popped her head into the reception area. "Good afternoon, John. Do you want to come with me?"

John stood up, the corners of his mouth rising the moment he saw her. "Yep, no worries. My favourite part of the day, when I get to see you," he chuckled.

Emily could feel heat rising up her neck. She was doing her best not to show this guy he was making her blush. She could do this. She could hold it together and show him how confident she was. She opened the door, stood back and let him walk into the room first, which gave her a few seconds to calm her speeding heartbeat. She sat down and started looking through her paperwork, buying herself some time before she had to lift her head and look directly at him. And breathe… Oh my God, he looked even better than the last time she'd seen him: clean-shaven, his big blue eyes staring at her. Come-to-bed eyes, he had, and she got lost in them for a few seconds before she spoke.

"How's things, John?" She sat twiddling her biro around in her fingers, waiting on his reply.

"It's been good. I've had a few days' work here and there, but nothing to write home about. The guy keeps saying he will have full-time work for me any time soon, but I think he's chatting shit. He just rings me to do a bit of shit-shifting, you know, on the building site."

Her voice felt too high: "Oh, that's great. At least you've got your foot in the door, so to speak. Fingers crossed, eh?"

John nodded slowly, blatantly looking her up and down. The cheek of this man! But there was no way she was getting embarrassed this time – she would stand her ground and not let him intimidate her. Truth be told, if it had been any other man she'd have pulled him up on it, maybe even filed a report. But there was no way she was reporting John Spencer – she knew if any attention was shone on him her colleagues would see right through her straight away and notice how she blushed just saying his name.

But, instead of talking more about his work prospects, he surprised her. "I've got a new tattoo. Do you want to see it?" Before she could reply, he stood up and lifted his t-shirt above his stomach to where a series of words ran sinuously below his heart. Oh my God, those bloody abs again – prison abs, she couldn't help thinking – and the tanned body sprinkled with dark hairs which trailed towards his belt. She instinctively licked her lips. She squinted as she tried to read the words on the tattoo.

"It says 'Carpe Diem'. It means 'seize the day' in Latin. And, I mean, that's what it's about for me lately, seizing opportunities and running with them."

"It's er… well, it's not what we're here to discuss, but it's a lovely sentiment, John. I like the meaning. You are right about seizing the day. You never know what's around the corner, do you?" She was away with the fairies now, thinking about days gone by and chances she'd missed.

"Penny for them," he chuckled.

Emily was back in the moment, embarrassed that she'd been caught out. "Sorry. I was thinking about those words. They make great sense, and seeing them each day should motivate you not to give up."

"I never give up, Emily. You'll find with me that if I want something I will strive to get it, no matter what it is."

Was he talking in double meanings now, talking about how he felt about her? She wasn't sure, but there was a gleam in his eye, that much was clear. She'd hoped last time he'd simply caught her on a bad day – that he'd arrive today and she'd realise she'd been a fool. But seeing him again, one thing she was sure about was that she fancied the hell out of this guy. All night long she'd been thinking about him, imagining him in her bed, making love with him, kissing every inch of that tight toned body he had. He'd awakened something in her and she only hoped it wasn't written all over her face.

"What about your home situation, John, how are you doing with that? I know the last time we spoke about your housing you had a few problems? I'm hoping that they have subsided and aren't a problem anymore?"

John sat back in his seat and locked eyes with her again. "Yeah, all sorted now. I had a word with the landlord and told him, if he didn't do the repairs, I would be reporting him, and he soon seen the light. Shit himself, he did. The next day he was in fixing the window and the leaking radiator."

"That's brilliant. See, it's all coming together for you now. I'm happy you are finding your feet."

There was a loaded silence between them, and they stared at each other across the table. In her mind, she was slowly peeling off his shirt, kissing him like she'd never kissed a man before. She'd heard from her friends who'd got divorced and found love again, about the heat of lust after a drought, and what it does to a woman. And here she was, for the first time in her married life, wanting to pounce on a guy and show him what she was about. She felt alive inside again, desires taking over every inch of her body and there was not a thing she could do to stop them. Archie was not really interested in sex anymore and, to be quite honest, neither was she. Her desire sort of petered out over the time they were together. One minute they were all over each other like two horny rabbits, and the next her sex life had become dull and routine. Then, gradually, even that had disappeared. Maybe it was because he had let her down. Went with another woman behind her back and broke her heart. She told herself she'd forgiven him, but in her heart there was a hole where it had not repaired. She supposed that was the problem when you had a cheating partner, wasn't it? You forgive them, but you also lose respect for them. If they'd loved you like they said they loved you, they would never have had their heads turned in the first place. For months after the affair, she read book after book about infidelity. Blaming herself, doing everything in her power to make their marriage work and, in all fairness, it did work. They got back on track, but the memory of him with another woman was never far from her thoughts. Even worse, it was a woman she knew, a woman she could never rid her mind of. It was many years ago, firmly in the past, she'd thought. She reached for a sip of cold water, then carried on with the meeting, ticking boxes and filling forms out. John never took his eyes from her. He was like a tiger sizing up his prey, ready to attack.

The meeting was nearly at an end when John made his move, seizing the day just like his tattoo said. "If you fancy a friendly drink after work, I'd like that a lot. Emily, you can't hide that you like me too. I can see it in your eyes every time you look at me."

How on Earth could he tell she fancied him? Was it that obvious? She bit down hard on her lip. Why should she not have some fun before it was too late? She owed it to herself to balance the scales between her and her husband, and – who knew? – a little slap and tickle could be exactly what she needed to revive her marriage. There was always a good tune played on an old piano, she reminded herself. Her breath was shallow, almost panting, and she knew she could not fight off this attraction any longer. He was on her mind every waking hour. Every night before she fell asleep, he was her last thought. Better to get it out of her system once and for all. Then she'd go back to her safe life, and Archie would be none the wiser, but she would know she'd been desired, and that alone might be enough to heal the old scars of his infidelity. Her words fired out without any further hesitation. "Alright then, but just a friendly drink, nothing more. It has to be out of the way too, because I can't chance anybody seeing me. I can finish work early and meet you after, if that's alright? I'll be in my car." There, she'd said it. The ball was in his court now.

"Nice one. I'll wait at the shop on the main road, and you can pick me up there. We can drive up in the hills, if you want, grab a bite to eat."

"Yes alright, I'll be there around three o'clock. But I'm not hanging around."

John knew the meeting was over, and he'd got what he'd come for, by the look of him. His smile was bigger than ever as he made to leave the room. "I'll tell you what, Emily, this tattoo is already bringing me luck. See you at three bells. Looking forward to it." He left, and she was alone.

She piled her papers together and sat thinking. She was putting a lot on the line here: her job, her marriage. She should feel terrible, but at this moment she didn't seem to care. One life, and she was living it. Finally doing what she wanted rather than what other people expected her to do. Balls to them all.

She went back to the main office and flicked through her emails. But nothing was registering. As time passed, doubt started to creep in. Maybe she should ring him and say she'd made a mistake, tell him she was a happily married woman in a trusted job with firm rules. Or maybe she could simply not turn up. But he would be stood waiting for her, gutted if she never turned up. Perhaps it was best to go and have one drink with him to tell him this is where it ends. Right now, she wished she was more like her middle sister, Teresa. She was confident, fearless, knew how to treat men, knew how to get what she wanted, and never thought twice about anything.

Emily packed her stuff away and made to walk out of the office. Sod's law: Nancy was looking straight at her and then over at the clock. Emily picked up speed, but it was too late – Nancy was at her side.

"Oh, I didn't know you were finishing early. There is nothing down in the diary?"

Emily was in a panic. She knew the rules and anyone who had holiday or was finishing early had to log it down in the thick black diary that sat at the end of Nancy's desk. She had to front this out, make it look like there had been an oversight.

"Oh, didn't I write it down, love? Bloody hell, I thought I did. I'll come over now and log it. I've got a doctor's appointment that I forgot about. Brain dead I am, sometimes."

"No worries, let's fill it out now. Be more than my job's worth if the big-wigs come into the office and staff are missing without proper procedure. I'll be in the firing line for not knowing where staff are, and we don't want that, do we?"

Emily bit back the answer she really wanted to give, trotted to Nancy's desk and opened the diary at today's date. Her hand was shaking slightly as she scribbled down that she had a doctor's appointment. "There you go, love, all correct. You can sleep tonight now, can't you," she added sarcastically.

Nancy gawped, aware Emily was being smart – so out of character for her usually meek colleague. "Only doing my job, love."

Emily got her belongings and hooked her bag over her shoulder. "See you tomorrow." She picked up speed as she headed for the door. She was sweating, all hot and flustered, and she knew if she hesitated now she would never get the courage to do anything like this again.

A cold blast of wind hit Emily's face as she stepped out onto the street. She quickly buttoned up her blazer. Once she was in her car, reality set in – what was she doing? She struggled to put her seatbelt on, hands shaking, taking forever. She took a breath, reached into her handbag and pulled out her lip-gloss. As she applied it in the rear-view mirror, her hands still trembled and she mumbled to herself, "Right, breathe, girl, sort yourself out. You're carrying on like you're meeting a bleeding high court judge or something. He's a man, nothing more, nothing less. It's a drink – nothing heavy." She turned the engine over and pulled the handbrake off. As she headed out onto the main road, she surveyed the area. The last thing she needed was someone spotting her. She didn't know what she was more anxious about – getting seen by someone from work, or word getting back to Archie. She'd spent her life sticking to the rules and yet here she was, crossing the line.

She put the radio on low as she drove along the busy road, her eyes vigilant. The shop was coming up on her left, and her heart beat faster than ever. Oh my God, he wasn't there. She scanned the empty pavement. He'd stood her up. What a fool she'd made of herself. She drove a little further down the road. Already she was slagging him off in her mind, and herself too. Maybe it was for the best. But hold on, there – a man stepping out onto the road. She screwed up her eyes, trying to focus. It was him; he'd turned up after all. Her heart thundered. She flicked the indictor on and pulled over, trying to look calmer than she felt. The passenger door opened, and John jumped in.

He oozed confidence. "Bleeding freezing out there."

"I thought you were going to wait at the shop – I almost drove off?" Emily stuttered, wondering how different things would have been if she'd driven past.

"Yeah, I was, but there's a load of pissheads stood drinking there and I couldn't be arsed with them, so I walked down a bit."

Emily put the indicator on and pulled out to join the main traffic.

John clipped his seatbelt on, and she could feel his eyes all over her. "Where do you want to go, then? I'm easy."

She kept her eyes on the road and replied, still in a state of shock, "We can go up in the hills, if you want. I know a few pubs up near Dovestone Reservoir. It's beautiful up there – peaceful."

"Yep, you're the boss."

Emily inhaled his aftershave, a fresh, soapy fragrance, undeniably sexy. He'd changed too, clearly making an effort, and now he was wearing a smart light blue shirt and a pair of dark blue jeans. He looked nice. More than nice, she hated to admit. She was used to seeing him in his trackies, his casuals.

She smiled over at him. "It was a nightmare getting out of work. One of my colleagues asked where I was going. I had to think on my feet – you and I are both in big trouble if someone clocks us."

He chuckled, and patted her knee. "You're the kind of woman worth getting in trouble for. I'm so glad you agreed to meet me. Honest, I can't get you out of my head. It's like you are my drug and I'm addicted."

"Oh, stop it, you'll have me blushing," she purred, smiling despite herself. She wasn't used to people being this upfront.

"No, I'm serious. Think about it – I've been seeing you every week for at least four months and it's the best part of my week. All those hours – I reckon we've both got a sense of each other – and I think we both know there's chemistry. You're the best part of my week – I hope that's true for you, too."

Emily blushed again, but her heart was slowing now and she was starting to relax. "Have you been in a relationship recently, John? You don't have to tell me if you don't want…"

He shifted in the seat. "Well, none of them worth talking about. You know I've spent a lot of time locked up and no bird is going to wait around for me longer than a few months. Don't get me wrong, I've met girls when I've already been in the slammer, and they used to come and see me, but after a few times they ghosted me."

Emily looked puzzled. "How can you meet a girl when you're in jail, if you don't mind me asking?"

He winked at her. "Mobile phones, dating apps, Facebook, Instagram. Yes, I know we're not meant to do any of that shit, but all the inmates meet women like that. Honest, I was talking to about ten girls at once when I was serving my last sentence. You've got to do something to pass the time on the inside – and trust me, there are worse things you could be doing than cruising the dating apps."

Emily raised her eyebrows. "Despite my line of work, I guess I'm a little bit naive sometimes about life behind jail walls. My focus is on helping people move on from what happened on the inside, rather than dwelling on their sentences. I've heard some stories, though, stuff that doesn't sit too well with me. Gave me nightmares for months."

"Yep, jail is not a nice place to be, but you adapt to prison life after a few months. Mind you, it's home from home for some convicts, they're in so often, and for others it's the only place they feel safe – three meals a day, no bills to pay – easy life really when you think about it compared to some of the choices they face outside. I'm done though – I'm not looking to go back down for anything or anyone. That's why I kept a low profile – I was better off chasing women online than spending my sentence trying to play Billy Big Bollocks and running the wing." John looked out of the window but carried on. "It never came to much though, like I said. And as for relationships on the outside, you might not think it, but I've had my heart broken in the past. I met a girl once and I was really into her. Proper pretty, she was, like a model. I was even going to put a ring on her finger and buy a house together, but it went tits up. She was banging my mate behind my back. I caught them in bed together when they thought I was out of town. On my life, if I close my eyes, I can still see them when I walked in on them. It sends my blood cold. I mean, look at the hairs on my arm standing on end." He rubbed his hand along his arm, and he wasn't lying: he had goose-pimples.

"Cheating partners are the worst. And you're not alone. I've faced it, too."

John looked intrigued and was hanging on her every word, but Emily clammed up. John started to sing along to the radio, a rich and husky voice. Sometimes music said more than words could.

John went straight to the bar when they arrived at the pub, which was set back into the hills with a prime view down over the surrounding countryside. Emily went and found a quiet spot, and sat enjoying the peace that came from leaving the inner city behind. There was no way she was having more than one glass of wine. She was driving and glad of the excuse to keep a straight head. John sat next her as he placed the drinks on the table.

"Cushdy here, isn't it. Look at that open fire."

John looked over at the fire and smiled. "It's like watching ribbons of gold dancing about, isn't it? Look, every second the colours change and spin like a dancer, swaying one way then the other."

Emily leaned forward to get a better look. "I've never heard it described like that before, but you're right." She was glad of the chance to stare at the flames rather than lock eyes with John and admit the heat she felt wasn't all from the fire.

"When I was in jail, I signed up to a creative writing course – thought it might be a doss, I admit, but I got into it and the tutor said I wrote some good stories. Poems, too. I think writing is a kind of therapy. You can be who you want, say what you want, and nobody can judge you. Mind you, I've not written anything for a while. Don't look so surprised, there's lots you don't know about me!"

"It's true. I never had you down as a writer. You don't seem the sort."

"What, because I'm a criminal it means I can't have hobbies like normal people? Can't have a voice?"

She'd hit a nerve and quickly backpedalled. "No, I mean... don't take this the wrong way, but you look like a stereotypical man's man, not someone who would sit down and write. Not many of my clients sit in front of me and talk about poetry, I'll be honest. It's like if you said you liked baking cakes."

He laughed. "I'm a top baker, too, as it happens. See, I'm full of surprises. When I was in jail, one of the first times, I signed up for the cookery programme. I'm not just a pretty face, you know. I have lots more hidden talents. What about you, what do you like? I bet you're into craft and knitting and stuff like that."

Emily scoffed. "What, because I'm old you think I should be knitting?"

He winked at her, his point made. "See how we all stereotype people? Nothing wrong with knitting, but I said it so you could see my point of view. Anyway, go on, tell me about you and what you like. What really floats your boat?"

Emily was on the spot. He was staring at her as she sat thinking. Her mind was blank. She didn't even know herself. Was she boring, then? She'd spent so long looking after everyone else, she didn't have time for proper hobbies. She smiled. "I like music. All different kinds. And I like going to the theatre." See, she *was* interesting and *did* have a life. But when was the last time she even listened to any music? And as for theatre, she'd not been for years.

"I love music, too." John leaned forward. "Whenever I get a chance, I put the tunes on. Who do you listen to?"

Now, this was a hard one – she didn't want to seem like an old codger, saying someone he didn't know. "I like a bit of Ed Sheeran."

"Well, at least I've heard of him. He's alright."

The conversation flowed now and Emily felt the tension in her chest releasing. Age was just a number after all and, as they started to share their stories, it slipped from her mind that he was at least a decade younger than her. So what if anyone watching would have called her a cougar – there were worse things to be called.

John reached over and held her hand. Their eyes met and Emily felt like the rest of the world fell away. Was it him who leaned in or was it her? She wasn't sure. But their lips connected and they shared a soft kiss. Then Emily pulled away and gazed out of the window. She looked down at her wedding ring. Its shine seemed to fade, making it dull. She was a tart now, a hussy, a player. How could she lose herself to the moment, when this one moment could wreck the life she knew? This was meant to be revenge on Archie, a liberation for her – but suddenly it all felt a lot more complicated.

John touched her arm as if he could tell this was a whole new ball game for her. "We are just two people who are attracted to each other, Emily. Sometimes it happens and there is nothing anybody can do to stop it."

Her voice was shaky. "I've never done anything like this. I've always said people who cheat on partners are lower than a snake's belly."

"Yes, you might be right, but did you say your husband cheated on you? Call this a score settled."

But Emily could feel a tight band of anxiety gripping her chest. If she couldn't calm herself, she knew she would have a panic attack. She stood up. "I need to go to the loo." She rushed past him.

At the mirror, she straightened her hair. "Bleeding hell, Emily, what the hell are you doing, woman? Think about this before it's too late. Think about it." She turned the tap on and washed her hands, staring down at the running water. She didn't want all the years to flow away like that. She lifted her head, pulled her shoulders back and smiled at her reflection. "If it's good enough for him, then it's good enough for me. Come on girl, live your life. 'Carpe Diem'."

The time flew, and it felt like moments rather than hours before Emily realised she had to get home. The drive back sped by. Soon, the car came to a halt and John pointed at his flat. "There it is, my gaff, second floor, the one on the left. If you fancy a coffee, we can go up, but no pressure."

Emily already knew this was a no for her. The clock was ticking and she had to make her way home. She was already fifteen minutes late. "Thanks, John, for a great time. It was just what I needed. I won't come in for a coffee. I need to go home and sort tea out." It felt strange to even think of her normal life waiting for her at home.

"No need to explain. I want to thank you for what has been probably the best date I've ever had."

Emily smiled like a Cheshire cat and rolled her eyes. "Yeah, whatever," she chuckled.

"No, seriously. I'm telling the truth. No one I've dated has come close to you – a proper lady, you are, a strong woman."

She looked deep into his eyes and, if she could have had her own way, she would have been straight in his flat and finishing her night off with him. But she was a married woman. She had someone to answer to, and a lot of thinking to do about what she wanted. His warm fingers stroked her cheek and slowly he moved in for another kiss. This was more than a kiss, this was a connection, a bond they shared. Married or not, she was in deep now.

Chapter Seven

Teresa sneaked in through her front door and quickly locked it behind her, trying to keep her panic at bay. She'd had call after call from Gavin Turner demanding she got in touch with him, but she blanked him, turned her phone off. She couldn't bear to hear his chilling voice down the end of the blower issuing threats she knew he wouldn't hesitate to carry out. Bending, she looked at the post on the 'Home Sweet Home' door mat. This was far from her home anymore. She didn't feel safe here. Every slight noise, she jumped out of her skin. Every car that went by, she was up at the curtains, twitching from behind them. She hadn't been home for days because Gavin was looking for her. If she popped back to get something, she was straight in and out, knowing her neck was on the line. She was lucky to have a few friends, otherwise she would have been sleeping on the streets to keep herself safe. What she would give for a good night's sleep in her own bed. One by one, she flicked through the letters. She paused as she came to one that was handwritten. She rushed to the living room and sat down on the sofa with the letter unopened in her hand. She kicked off her high heels and tucked her feet underneath her. Minding her perfect manicure, she slid a long talon under the envelope's flap to open it and pulled out the letter. With wide eyes, she read every word, concentrating. Before she could fully take in the meaning of this message from her father, after so many years of nothing, her thoughts were interrupted by hammering on the door. Instinctively diving out of sight, she slid off the sofa and covered her head with a cushion. A voice outside sent chills down her spine. It was the voice she dreaded, the man she knew would end her life without a second thought, if that's what his orders were. It was one of Gavin's foot-soldiers. And if he was knocking, Gavin's patience was running out.

"I'll keep coming back, Teresa. You know it's only a matter of time before I get my hands on you. Do yourself a favour and pay what you fucking owe. The next time I come here I won't be knocking on your front door. Do you get the message, bitch? You better had. Gavin says it's payback time."

Teresa lay frozen, not moving a muscle. She had to sort this, fix it, before her life was over. Nowhere was safe anymore. And it wasn't only Gavin's heavies she had to worry about. Gavin Turner would end her himself if he got the opportunity. He was an evil bastard and she'd heard stories about how he tortured anyone who crossed him. If she didn't get the money, it would be no biggie for him to take her somewhere and batter her to death. And who would miss her? She'd be another beaten woman without a family to search for her, another missing sex worker for the papers to sneer at. No, she had to do something, and fast, if she wanted to avoid being just another crime number. When it was all quiet, she peeped over the arm of the sofa. She could see the front door through a small gap in the curtains. Slowly, slowly she sat up. She was safe for now. The bloke was gone, but surely not for long. She ran up the stairs and peered out onto the street. There was no sign of him. She fell back onto the bed and lay staring at the ceiling. This was it – she could give up and wait for him to come back, or she could fight, and fight harder and dirtier than she had ever done before.

She reached for her mobile phone and took a big breath before she began typing:

> Dear Teddy, I'm so sorry but I'm desperate and can't think of any other way out. Can you loan me some money until I'm back on my feet? Ten thousand pounds is what I need. I hope you can sort this for me as I can't see another way out. Love T xxxx

She examined the text, read it through again and again, then pressed the send button. She glanced at the photograph beside her bed and her vision blurred. Her son, her only child. She picked the photograph up and held it to her chest. "I still love you, Joel. I've never stopped loving you, but it was for the best you went to live with your dad. He could look after you, give you everything you needed." She tried to fight the tears back, but they burst out from her as the emotion of the day finally caught up with her. She was so tired. But the thought of her boy spurred her on. Joel was never far from her thoughts, and she had always regretted giving him up . But her lifestyle, her job, would never let her be a stay-at-home mother, and there was no time for looking after kids when she was earning the money she was earning. She'd told herself she'd pocket enough to get somewhere nice to live, and to stop turning tricks, then she'd get him back. But it had never worked out like that. Anyway, Joel's dad was loaded. And, sure, maybe she shouldn't have turned up on his doorstep with his son and let the cat out of the bag to his wife, but she had been at her wits' end when she handed him over. No money, no one to look after him and nowhere else to turn.

She'd left all her details with him, and Joel had written to her over the years, even sent a few photographs, but slowly the letters stopped, and she'd not had the balls to go and see him after that. She didn't want him dragged into her world, and she always had one hundred and one reasons why she shouldn't go to see him. He was settled and happy. Why would she ever spoil that for him? Giving him up was the worst thing she could have done – and the best thing she ever did for him.

A text alert. She rummaged around the bed to grab her phone. This could be it – her ticket out of here. She quickly read the message and snarled at the screen. "You cheeky bastard, Teddy." She flicked to her photographs and selected the ones of Spencer in the hotel room, naked. She'd given him a chance to help her, and he'd chosen not to. Even had the gall to tell her to delete his number. Maybe he needed reminding about his filthy little secret. She sent the photographs and this time her message was blunt. She wasn't proud, but she didn't have time to hang about.

> I need ten grand, otherwise I will send these to your lovely wife. You wouldn't want that, would you, Ted?

There were no kisses on this message, straight to the point. Teddy Mason was a wealthy man, he was always telling her about how much cash he had, so he needed to dig deep in his pocket and help her out, just like she did for him, in her own way.

Her mobile started ringing: Ted's number flashing on the screen. She sat up straight as she answered the call. She held the phone away from her ear as Teddy's desperate voice shrilled. "Now, now Ted. You need to calm down before you give yourself a bloody heart attack. All I need is some money. Call it a loan, because you will get every penny back." She cringed as she listened to the voice screaming down the phone again. "Well, the ball is in your court, honey-bunch. I tried asking you nicely, so now I've had to up my game. I thought you really cared about me, Teddy. You said you would take me on holiday, said you would buy me clothes, but none of that has ever happened.

If you ever cared about me at all, then do this to save me. I'm in serious bother, Ted, deep shit. But, if you won't do it to save me, then do it to save your marriage. I ain't messing about." She held the phone away again as she listened to him spit venom. She was warming up now. "I had feelings for you, and I thought you felt the same." She listened to his excuses a bit longer then went in for the kill. "I'm doing this to protect you too, in a funny way. I mean, these men, if they don't get their money back from me, what do you think they'll do next? They know I've got some wadded clients. It won't take them long to come knocking at your door." The yelling at the other end stopped. She smiled to herself as she listened to his voice getting reasonable now. Once he'd finished, she coughed to clear her throat. "Meet me tonight at the Old Church at eight o'clock with the money. I don't want to print these photographs out and send them to your wife. I don't want to be doing any of this, but trust me, I've got no choice. And don't be thinking about any funny business, Teddy-boy, because my friend has a copy of them, and I've told her, if anything happens to me, to send them straight to your wife *and* the police."

The call ended and Teresa let out a shaky breath. She held her phone in her hands and searched for Emily's number. She stared at the screen, looking at the name. She thought about how her sisters had always made everything better, when they were younger. They'd faced hell – but they'd done it together. And in between the hard times, there had been happy times too. Teresa had liked cooking when she was growing up, often baked with her mum and her sisters on a Sunday afternoon. The four of them would make cheese and onion pies, steak pies, apple crumble, jam tarts. They were her good memories of home, the ones she chose to keep. There were other memories that she'd shut away and never ever opened again. They caused her too much pain, made her cry. But she wished she had her sisters here with her now. Teresa had always been the go-between, bridging the gap between Emily as the eldest and most sensible, and Shannon as the baby of the family. Her finger hovered over the call button, but the thought of having to tell Emily the truth about the mess she'd got into made her stop. Instead, she would do what she always did when she was down on her luck. Scrub herself up, put on her make-up. Whatever was going to happen, she would face it looking gorgeous.

Teresa brushed her hair and sprayed her Black Vanilla perfume over her body. She always felt clean when she smelt the sweet coconut fragrance. It reminded her of holidays, the good times when money wasn't a problem and the world was her oyster. She only had a few squirts of the perfume left, so she chose carefully when she wore it. She could never pay the price of the fragrance now she was skint. She touched up her nails, then added a fresh lick of lipstick and eyeliner as sharp and black as her thoughts. Then she made her way downstairs, flinching at every sound. She was a sitting duck and she knew it – time to get out of here. The clock was ticking. She was dressed in black skinny jeans and a tight knitted black polo neck. She wanted to blend into the night, not draw any attention to herself. She looked at the sharp silver knife on the table and slid it into her handbag. If necessary, she would use it. She had in the past. She would do anything to save her own life.

In her line of work, women were never safe when they were working. When she was younger, she found herself in some really bad situations and feared for her life more than once. Often it was the customers you least expected that caused the most danger. She remembered the worst time. It was a normal late-night party at a hotel room with a group of rowdy men. She'd been to lots of these bookings and, in all fairness, she had earned over a grand in one night keeping these men happy. The men were drug-fuelled and had way too much to drink. It started when she heard her friend Cathy screaming from one of the bedrooms and she rushed in to see if she was alright. That was the rule when you did in-calls with a friend: you always had each other's back. As she'd opened the door, she could see her friend scrambling to the other side of the room and the two men looking at each other. She'd run to her side, cradled her in her arms, trying to find out what had happened. And that's when her head went crashing into the wall with the force of a kick from one of the men. Another man grabbed her by the throat. She'd pulled out the small knife that she'd shoved down her long black boots and went to town on the men. She sliced them both across the face, dug the blade into their legs. She and Cathy had run from that hotel like women possessed and, afterwards, both admitted they were lucky to be alive. At first, she'd been terrified of them coming after her, but they hadn't had to wait long before the same two men were arrested for murder – another couple of working girls that could have so easily been them. Since that night Teresa never went anywhere without being tooled up. It was a dangerous world out there and she would never be caught off guard again. Not now, not ever.

Teresa stood in the shadows of the night outside the Old Church. It was a dilapidated building and had been derelict for as long as she could remember. Smackheads used its ground to sleep in. Prostitutes took their clients there; other people moved in the shadows, and you didn't look too closely if you knew what was good for you. Teresa examined the crumbling church in more detail and wondered what it had looked like in its day. The bricks were black now, the roof bare of any slates, like a set from a horror film. She stood back a few steps and blended into the background. Her heartbeat doubled as she spotted a black car moving slowly along the roadside. She dipped her head and zipped her coat up. It was him: do or die time.

Ted Mason pulled up at the side of her and, even before she climbed in, his voice was down her ear. "I'll make sure none of my friends use you again after this. *Discreet service* you have always told me, but now I know the truth: you are a blackmailing bitch."

Teresa sat down in the passenger seat and tried her best to keep her voice low. "I asked you to help me and you told me never to contact you again. How dare you treat me like I'm a dollop of dog shit on the bottom of your shoe. You told me I was special, said I was the best you have had. Do anything for me, you said."

"I did want to help, but ten bleeding grand? Are you having a laugh? I can't pull that kind of money out of thin air."

She glanced at a brown envelope on his lap. "Teddy, I'll pay every penny back. I've got myself into a bit of debt and I have some nasty geezers knocking on my door, threatening to do this and that to me." She flicked her hair back from her face. "Look at me, look into my eyes. You are the only person who can help me. I have nobody, no family, no friends, no one."

Teddy was calming down, but he wouldn't look at her. "It's my own fault for even getting myself into situations like this. My secret, my karma, I suppose."

Teresa put her hand on his knee and squeezed it gently. "I'm sorry. You mean so much to me and, when you told me you weren't going to help, I lost my head. I love you, Teddy. I've never told you this before, but in my heart I hoped you felt something for me too." She watched him from the corner of her eye as she sat playing with her fingers. She snivelled and forced tears. She was giving a performance any leading actress would be proud of. He shuffled about in his seat nervously.

Slowly, he slid the envelope onto her lap but kept a tight grip on it. "I want the photographs gone."

Teresa pulled her mobile phone out and searched her photographs. She showed them to him and one by one she deleted them.

"What about the ones your friend has, the ones you said would go to the police if anything happened to you?"

"They will be deleted once I have counted the money. You have my word on that, and I stick to my word."

Teddy was flapping, small beads of sweat forming on his forehead. He looked deep into her eyes now. "Promise me, this is the end of this? I will not be able to live with myself if my wife ever gets wind of this."

She patted his shoulder, and swallowed hard. "This will be the end of it. I promise you. And as soon as I get back on my feet, I will start paying you back. In fact, any time we meet in the future will be free, so every cloud has a silver lining, doesn't it? I mean, you still want to see me, don't you? For that special thing you like?"

Teddy was all hot and flustered, rubbing slowly at his crotch. All the blood running from his brain to his manhood, not thinking straight. "Well, of course I'll still be coming to see you. Bloody hell, I would go mental if I didn't have my time with you each week. I'll draw up some sort of account, and I might be coming to see you twice a week now that I've already paid for it."

Teresa pulled the envelope slowly from his hand and made to leave the car. He pulled her back softly and chuckled. "What about a suck before you go? Now I've paid up?"

Teresa wriggled free, got out of the car and bobbed down so she could see him. "Not tonight, love. There's a price on my head and no one's safe til I've sorted it. I've got to go and settle a few things, then you can call me whenever you like."

She slammed the car door shut and headed off down the road, hanging onto the money for dear life. She knew what men like Ted were like, double-crossing, setting her up, ringing the dibble if he thought he could get away with it. Teresa walked down the dimly lit road and reached into her coat pocket for a cigarette. Her heart was in her mouth, and she kept looking over her shoulder.

Teresa had been walking for at least ten minutes. She stopped to survey the dark field facing her. She had a choice now; she could cut across the field or add an extra fifteen minutes onto her journey. This place had been all over the news, how men had been reported lurking in the darkness waiting to attack women. But she felt danger all around her already. She stepped onto the muddy grass and her choice was made. She had her knife with her and, if any prick stepped within an inch of her, she would stick it in them. Whoever might be in the shadows couldn't be as bad as Gavin and his boys. But a few minutes later, she already regretted taking the short cut. Branches crunching behind her, mind playing tricks with her, shadows coming alive moving towards her. Thick clouds of steam left her mouth as she picked up speed – noises in the distance – and then ahead, finally, lights spraying onto the field from the main road. Her heartbeat started to settle, she stopped looking behind her, she was nearly safe. Teresa placed her hand inside her leather jacket and smiled as she gripped the envelope. All her problems were over now – she would pay off Gavin and she could start to breathe again.

Suddenly she felt a hot burning in her side. She was dragged one way then the other, and then she was falling. Cold mud. A man's voice. Eyes looking down at her as a fist pummelled into her face. Before she could cry out, a hand covered her mouth. She felt his other hand rummaging inside her clothes. Cold, rough skin against hers. Was this rape? She tried to shout against the gagging hand, but no words came out. As she finally focused in the gloom, she saw her attacker's eyes staring down at her, a smirking, evil look.

"Scruffy old bitch, who the fuck do you think you are, demanding money from people?" He booted her in the stomach. Then his warm tobacco breath was in her face again. Teresa could barely move as she felt him yank the envelope out of her pocket. Without a backward glance at her, he gripped the envelope and jogged away with his hood up, clearly knowing which route to take, which cameras to avoid. Silence.

Teresa rolled onto her side and her face creased with pain as she dug her long fingernails into the thick black mud, trying to push herself upright. "Bastard," she groaned. After what seemed like forever, she managed to get onto all fours and sought refuge under a large oak tree, the thick brown branches hanging low, shielding her from the icy wind. She sat up straight and gasped for breath, her eyes flickering rapidly. Why the hell did she let herself get robbed? She hadn't even had chance to reach for her blade. And now she wasn't only back where she started, but even worse off. Her bottom lip trembled as she struggled to get her mobile phone from her jacket pocket. As she gripped it, a thought dawned on her, and she remembered what the guy had said as he laid into her. If this had just been a mugging, any opportunist thief would have taken her phone as well. No, this was a guy who knew what he was looking for. It was all a set-up. Teresa clenched her teeth: she should have known Teddy would have something up his sleeve for her. It had all been too easy. But Ted would pay for double-crossing her. Quickly, she unlocked her phone. With shaking hands, she scrolled through her recently deleted photographs and recovered them all.

"I'll show you now," she whispered. She typed out a new message:

> I'm still breathing, you fucking idiot. Now the price has gone up. I want twenty thousand pounds, you prick. Here are my bank details, you have until twelve o'clock tomorrow to send the money over. No more games. Pay up, or the wife will know what a seedy, dirty prick you really are.

She attached the photographs and sent them over to Teddy.

This was war, and she was willing to go all the way to get what she wanted. Twenty grand would give her serious options. With that kind of cash, she could vanish, make a fresh start. Fuck Gavin and the money she owed, he could whistle for it. It was time for change anyway, time to move properly away and leave her old life and troubles behind her. She'd done it before, and she could do it again. She sat under the tree and sparked a fag up. There was no rush to get home, or to get help. She had a plan, and she was trusting only herself to make it happen.

Big girls don't cry. They get even.

Chapter Eight

Shannon walked next to Paddy into Asda. He was never far from her side, like a bad smell. It was busy today and the shoppers were out in full force. Shannon was usually delighted to be out of the house, but not today. Everything still ached, and she felt ashamed going out in this state. Paddy had already told her they would be in and out of this place with only what *he* said they needed. That usually meant bread and milk and a few cans of Stella for him. She'd begged to be allowed to stay at home, told him she couldn't walk properly, but he'd told her to get her fucking coat on because she was coming with him. There was no talking to him when he was like that. It was his way or the highway. Paddy had no tolerance for what he called weak people. He hated that she cried when he shouted at her. Cry on the inside, he always told her, tears were for the puny.

Shannon stood on the spot twisting about, legs crossed. "I need a wee. Honest, I'm busting."

Her boyfriend growled at her and shook his head. "For crying out loud, woman, why didn't you have one before we came out?"

"I did. I need another one. I only need a bloody wee, for crying out loud." She knew she was overstepping the mark by the way he looked at her, his eyes wide, his nostrils flaring. She shot a look over at the toilets and raised her eyebrows at him. "You start to get the shopping and I'll catch up with you."

His voice was firm. "I'm staying put. Hurry the fuck up, woman."

Shannon hobbled to the toilets and entered a cubicle. Her eyes landed on the notice on the back of the door. It was a domestic violence contact number, people who could help a woman like herself. It felt like a sign. She read the full poster, once, twice and a third time. Rummaging in her coat pocket, she searched for a pen. There was usually an old chewed-up bookie's pen floating around in her pocket, but not today. She finished and flushed the toilet. She stood for a few seconds thinking before she unlocked the door. When she emerged, an oldish woman stood there looking at her. A friendly face, she reminded Shannon of her own gran – grey hair, round silver glasses hanging on a chain. Shannon knew time wasn't on her side and she panicked – if she didn't act now, she wouldn't get the chance again. Her words were stuttered. "Excuse me, love," Shannon mumbled. "Can I use your mobile phone to make a quick call?"

The shopper backed off and held her handbag with both hands. She stood back, voice trembling. "I don't have any money, love, and if you lay one finger on me I will scream at the top of my voice."

Shannon shook her head. She knew she didn't look like the kind of person you'd trust. "I'm not a robber. Believe me…" She quickly took her coat off and lifted her t-shirt revealing the purple and red bruises all over her body. "I need to phone for help. My boyfriend's done this to me. He's always hurting me, and I can't get away from him. There's a helpline on the back of the toilet door, and I want to phone the number. He's waiting outside for me and, if I don't hurry up, he'll be in here dragging me out. Please, let me get some help." Shannon quickly pulled her clothes back down.

The old woman was still trying to make her mind up, but she'd seen the bruises on this woman's body, and the sadness in her eyes. She stepped forward and placed her warm hand on Shannon's shoulder. "Of course you can, and, if that big idiot is outside waiting for you, I will give him a mouthful. How dare he place his hands on you? He's a bully, nothing more. If I was a few years younger, I would put him on his arse. A man that hits a woman is a coward, a bleeding coward."

The mobile phone was in Shannon's hands now. She trembled as she pressed each digit. She held the phone to her ear, waiting, praying somebody would answer her. An answer phone kicked in. It had to be worth a chance.

"Hello, my name is Shannon. I live at ninety-five Joshua Street near the Marsh Estate. Please help me to get away. He said he would kill me if I ever left him. Please, send somebody to help me." She gave a few more details and ended the phone call. She passed the phone back to the woman and smiled gently at her. "I will never forget your kindness. You might have saved my life."

Paddy was waiting right outside the toilets. He was clearly fuming. He checked his chunky silver watch and snarled at her, "For fuck's sake, how long does it take? You're lucky I never come in and grabbed you out of there. I've got places to go, people to see. Come on, move it." He gripped her arm and pulled her away from the toilets.

The shopping was done, and Paddy was rushing along the main road with his head down. It was cold today and his cheeks were bright red. They were always red from the beer he supped, but today they seemed to be on fire. Shannon trailed behind him, but Paddy was a man on a mission, he couldn't wait to get home and pick out some horses for a bet. He had the Racing Post tucked neatly under his arm. Often he would sit for hours studying the form, then tell everyone he met that day that he had a tip for them, a sure thing.

"I'm going to win us a fortune today, Shan. If my bet comes in, we'll be jetting off into the sunset, me and you. Do you fancy a bit of sunshine, or what?"

She couldn't care less where she was, to be honest, and all she was thinking about at this exact moment was going back to her home, her prison. Her sentence had no parole, no date circled on her calendar when she would be free. She was a lifer.

She swallowed hard before she replied. She could see his eyes burning into her, waiting on a reply. "Any sunshine would be nice. I'm sick of the weather around here."

Maybe she should run away now, while they were out in public where somebody could help her. But her body was weak, her energy low. And where could she go? Who would put their neck on the line and protect her from Paddy? None of her old friends would do it. She thought back to a night out with the girls years ago when she had stayed out longer than normal so she could party at the flat of one of her friends. Paddy nearly took the door from its hinges when he banged on it, looking for her. "Get my Mrs fucking out here now," he'd screamed at her friend Tracy.

Tracy was sick of the way this man spoke to his girlfriend. She'd witnessed it time and time again. The booze had given her courage, strength to give him a piece of her mind. Paddy listened to the lecture Tracy gave him and then he was like a bull in a china shop. Straight through the front door he stormed, throwing ornaments about, booting anything that got in his way, breaking the table, smashing pictures in their frames. And he wasn't finished there, either. He pointed his finger at everyone in the room and roared at them like a caged lion. "Anyone else got something to say?" Nobody moved a muscle, all huddled together, whispering. Paddy eyeballed the group and threatened that, if any of them hid his woman again, he would put them ten feet under. After that day, everyone gave Shannon a wide berth, scared of any aftermath of spending time with her, petrified that Paddy would boom their front door down and smash their gaff up.

No, Shannon could never run away to a friend's place. Maybe Teresa would put her up, help her in her time of need – but how would she get over to Burnley? And what if Teresa didn't even live there anymore? There was always Emily, but she doubted she would ever be welcomed over her doorstep. Didn't know if she could face it, either. Paddy had strangled the relationship between the sisters, but she knew she had made it easy for him, took any excuse not to face up to what she'd done. She could go to see her mother and father though, ask them for help. Didn't the letter prove that? They would never turn their backs on her. But Paddy wouldn't let her out of his sight. No, she'd have to go home and bide her time.

Back at the house, Paddy sat munching hot toast, slurping his cup of tea. He shot a look over at Shannon. "Where is your toast? I told you to get a couple of slices down your neck, because there is fuck all else in the fridge, and I'm not leaving you any money to grab something from the corner shop later or phone for food. I'm not made of money."

"I'm not hungry. Can't eat when I'm in pain, can I?" She sat down on the sofa and reached for the tablet bottle. She unscrewed the lid and shook two tablets into the palm of her hand. Her calmers, the only things that took away the feeling she held deep in her chest. Her anxiety was through the roof and crippling every inch of her body. Paddy let out a laboured breath. "You can knock them tablets on the head after that bottle. You're like a bleeding zombie, woman, always away with the fairies. Get a few voddies down your neck instead of being a pill-popper. It isn't attractive, you know?"

She panicked, wriggling nervously on the sofa. Scared he would take her medication from her, make her go cold turkey, let her rattle. He was more than capable of doing that. He'd done it before for two days when they fell out. He'd told her he hoped she'd die without them.

Desperately, she replied, "I need these tablets. The doctor prescribes them for my anxiety, to help me calm down. You can't just stop taking medication without the doctor's say so."

"What bleeding anxiety? Fuck all wrong with you, woman, nothing that I can't cure anyway. You need a leg-over, that's all, and I can help with that before I go out, if you want?" He winked at her and rubbed at his crotch.

She pulled her brown cardigan tightly around her body and brought her knees up to her chest. The thought of her partner rolling about on her made her feel sick in the pit of her stomach. He was like an animal during sex: rough, yanking her hair, biting her body, no tenderness whatsoever. "I'll give it a miss, thank you very kindly. I'm going to have a few hours' sleep and try and get my head together."

Paddy looked around the living room and folded his newspaper on the arm of the chair. "You can give this place a good clean. It's a right shit tip. Look at all the clothes piled high. Lazy cow, you've turned into. Bone idle."

Just as she was tempted to give him a mouthful, there was a knocking at the front door, loud insistent banging.

Paddy got up, a puzzled look on his face. "Who the eck is that, knocking like we owe them money or something?"

Shannon sat up straight, stretching her neck to see if she could see who it was. Paddy pulled his t-shirt down over his pot belly and headed to answer it, closing the living room door behind him. Shannon jumped up and ran to the door to listen. Frank was at her feet, jumping up at her. "Move, Frank, bloody hell, go and lie down," she whispered down at him. She could hear raised voices, and she ran back to the sofa and sat down. The living room door swung open. She could see two police officers and another woman who was holding some paperwork in her hands. Shannon felt a wave of hope and fear all wrapped up in one.

Paddy stormed into the front room and stood over Shannon. "Look, there's fuck all wrong with her, so go back to whoever is giving you the information and tell them they are barking up the wrong tree here."

The officer walked further into the room, and you could see he was ready for trouble, eyes never leaving Paddy. His colleague was still in the hallway and already he was on the blower for back-up. Paddy was aggressive and his reputation meant every local copper had heard of him, but somehow they bundled him out into the hall.

The woman's voice was low as she sat down next to Shannon on the sofa. "Hello, I am Bernadette and I work for the domestic violence team. I have information that you need our help. Is that right?" Paddy was outside screaming at the top of his voice, trying to get near Shannon, but she could also hear the two officers: "Please calm down, sir. Let the lady answer for herself."

"You tell them, love, tell them someone is playing games and talking a load of shit behind our backs." The door swung open and Paddy stood there panting like some kind of wild animal. Shannon took a deep breath. The stage was hers now. She looked over at Paddy and the sight of him gave her the courage to carry on.

The woman could see she was nervous and gently patted her knee. "Just take your time. If you want to be alone to talk to me, then the officers will leave us alone?" She looked over at the officers and spoke directly to them. "Can you leave us alone? Paddy, can you go and wait in another room while I speak to Shannon?"

"It's a bleeding joke, all this. Me and the Mrs are fine."

The officer stood his ground and eyeballed Paddy. "Leave them to talk. If it's all as you say, then everything will be fine. We have a job to do so the quicker you let them get cracking the quicker we can go."

Paddy shot a look over at Shannon. "You tell them, love, tell them these nosey cunts are just poking their noses in."

He left the room followed closely by the two officers. Shannon never took her eyes from the door, her body shaking from head to toe. Frank jumped on the sofa and plonked himself on her lap, his big brown eyes looking up at her. She gently stroked her thin hand across his head. She felt better for his reassuring presence. Bernadette sat back and told Shannon she could take her time but she wanted to put her mind at rest first. "Shannon, we can get you help, find you a new home, keep you safe. If these allegations are true, then you owe it to yourself to get away from here and be happy. No man has the right to raise his hand to a woman. Whether it is physical abuse or mental abuse, it is not acceptable. You have a right to be happy and I am here today to make sure you have a choice."

Paddy could be heard from the other room, shouting, snapping.

Shannon rubbed at her arms. She swallowed hard, tears bursting from her eyes. Her words were slow, and she lifted Frank's head up gently, talking directly to him. "I told you I would get us help, boy, didn't I tell you I was sorting it?"

Bernadette smiled at her: she knew this woman was ready to open up and tell her exactly what had been going on.

Shannon helped Frank from her lap and stood up. Slowly, she raised her t-shirt, revealing the bruises. She turned around and let Bernadette see the rest of her injuries. There were old bruises still visible, too. "I need you to help me get away. Frank, too. I'm not going anywhere without my dog. He's saved me, he has, always been by my side when I had nothing else left."

Bernadette nodded and let Shannon carry on.

"I've been his prisoner for a long time now. He never leaves my side. He locks me in the house, leaves me freezing in here while he's out on the piss. And then he comes home and kicks ten bells out of me. It's the same every week. He gets pissed and goes to town on me."

"Do you have any family you can go and stay with, Shannon?"

"I have family, but we don't really speak anymore. My dad sent me a letter the other day telling me my mother is ill and he wants me to go and see her, but, apart from that, me and my two sisters very rarely talk. Shit happens in families, doesn't it?"

"Yes, it does, but I'm sure, if you told them what has being going on, they will welcome you with open arms."

"I wish it was that easy. I've hurt people in the past, one of my sisters especially, and although she said she has forgiven me, I know she hasn't. They both hate me and, to be honest, I hate myself too." She exploded with tears, sobbing her heart out. "I wish I could make it all better, wish it had never happened. I was young and foolish back then."

Bernadette passed her a tissue and gave her a few minutes to settle back down. "I can get you a bed at a women's refuge out of the area. It will be women like you who are staying there, people you can trust to help you recover, help you deal with what has happened."

"I'm a mess. I pop pills all day long to help blank it out. I've always took tablets to block things out. It's the way I have always coped."

"We can get you help with everything, Shannon. Do you want to get your things together and we can leave here?"

Shannon stared, aware Paddy was in the other room kicking off. "I don't have anything to take, only what I'm stood in. It's sad, isn't it, that my life amounts to fuck all, only these few rags, and Frank here, of course."

"Today is a new day for you, Shannon. We will get you all the help you need. We will help you start a new life.

You're stronger than you think – and once you take the first step, the rest will follow."

Paddy barged past the officers and sprinted back into the living room. Bernadette stood up and guarded Shannon.

He screamed, "So, have you told them to fuck off, told them we are fine?"

The officers were at Paddy's side now and they gripped him so he could not go further into the room. Shannon knew he would never take this lying down.

She pushed Bernadette out of the way and spoke to him. Her voice was calm, and she meant every word. "It's never been fine, Paddy, never been good. You have beat me within an inch of my life and treated me like a prisoner for years. I was actually starting to believe I was worthless like you told me I was, but, for the record, it is you who is worthless. I'm leaving you for good. I'm going to make something of my life and do all the things I've dreamed about. I've showed them the bruises all over me, Paddy, told them how you lock me in this bleeding house and keep me shut away like a prisoner. You're the one who should be in jail, not me."

Paddy was fighting to break free and the officer who had been called as back-up arrived just in time. They were all over him. They floored him and twisted him up, hands behind his back, handcuffs on. Shannon walked over to the table, picked up the dog's lead and clipped it to Frank's collar. "We're free, boy. Free from this nightmare." She made to walk past Paddy, but when she got to him she stopped and slowly bent down so she could look into his eyes. "Rot in hell. I'll show you what I can do. I will repair inside and out and be strong again. No man will ever treat me like you have again. Lesson learned."

He was actually frothing at the mouth. "Bitch, I'll find you, you know I will, and God help you when I do. I'll fuck you up good and proper. Nobody fucks with me, fucking nobody." His voice, that grating rasp which usually sent shivers down her spine, didn't sound so tough now.

She turned back one last time to look at him. With any luck, she'd never set eyes on him again.

Chapter Nine

"Mam, where is my black leather coat? You had it last. Why didn't you put it back in my wardrobe, then I wouldn't be screaming and shouting looking for it?"

Emily sat on the sofa, looking at her phone, and replied tiredly, "It's in my car. Bloody hell, it's not the end of the world. Shove your shoes on and go and get it. Lazy cow."

"You won't be borrowing anything of mine again, Mother. Sick of you lately nicking my clothes to wear. Go and buy your own."

Emily raised her eyes and carried on texting. She seemed relaxed today, not a care in the world.

Archie walked in and sat down on the sofa next to her, looking like a spare part. After a few minutes, he snuggled in closer to his wife. "If Jena is out tonight, we could do something special. Maybe even an early night, nudge-nudge, wink-wink?"

She wriggled about, moving Archie away from her. The thought of his hands over her body gave her the ick. "Erm,

I'm out tonight. I did tell you last week that the girls from work are meeting up for a few drinks. Did you forget?"

Archie scratched his head. "What again? Bloody hell, I thought you couldn't stand half of them. You're always slagging them off from the minute you walk through that front door each night. A bit two-faced, if you ask me."

She shoved her mobile phone into her pocket. "There are a few girls I don't get on with, granted, but you get that in every workplace. And, if I'm being honest, it's only since I've been going out more that you have noticed me again. Go on, when was the last time you asked me to do something special or have an early night? Too little too late, Archie."

He sighed and reached over to touch her hand, but she moved it away quickly. "Emily, where has all this come from? I've always made the effort with you. You're the one who carts me all the time. Maybe I just got sick of being black-balled. If you have a problem with me then bring it to the table and we can talk about it, sort it out and get back to how we used to be."

She let out a sarcastic laugh. "Like we used to be. Are you having a laugh? What, do you mean like the times I sat up all night waiting for you to come home, coming in at all hours stinking of perfume, stinking of her?" She'd said it now, brought it to the table, and he had to defend himself.

"Wow, how did I know you would bring this up? It's always the same with you, Emily, you never let sleeping dogs lie. You said you'd forgive me, that you would get over it in time. But how fucking long do you need? I tread on eggshells every day around you and do my best to make you happy, and all you do is throw it back in my face."

She was fuming, steam coming out of her ears. "Because some days, that's how I feel. I forgive you but I'll never forget. How could I?"

Jena walked into the room and shot a look at her parents, aware they were having beef. Emily tried to smooth it over like she always did around her daughter, and made small talk. "Where are you off to all dressed up? Do you have a date?"

Archie joined in the conversation. "If you are dating, then be careful. So many weirdos out there these days. Does he have a job? Where does he live?"

Jena blew a laboured breath. "You two do my head in. Who even said I was going out on a date? Stop jumping to conclusions. If I'm dating, then you two will be the first to know. I'm going out for food with Karis, so relax."

"Any sign of a job yet?" Emily asked.

"Actually, I've got a few jobs on the horizon, so put that in your pipe and smoke it."

Emily sat up straight, looking her daughter up and down. "So, if you're not working, where are all these new clothes coming from?"

Jena went beetroot. "I borrowed them from Karis. For crying out loud, you two are like the Gestapo."

"We ask because we care, sweetheart. How many times have we watched TV and seen some young woman get taken advantage of, or worse still, go missing? I know you are not a baby anymore but, while you are living under our roof, you stick to our rules, and that means telling us where you're going, and coming in at a decent hour, not rolling in with the milkman."

"Dad, it was only once I got in late. God, I can't wait to get my own house and then I can do what the hell I please."

Emily smirked and rolled her eyes. "Yes, and then you will come crashing down to Earth with a bang. Bills to pay, food to buy, you won't know what has hit you, girl."

Jena shot a look at her mother, the red mist descending. "I'm going out and don't worry, I will be in at a decent hour. You two want to worry about your own relationship instead of mine, anyway. I'm sick of you bickering all the time. That's your problem: you are bored because your lives are the same thing day in and day out. Try going out and having a few beers, go away for the weekend and give me a bit of bloody breathing space."

Jena flicked her hair over her shoulders and grabbed her red leather handbag from the sofa. "See you two pensioners later."

Archie piped up, "I'm staying in on my lonesome, love. Your mam is out again with the girls."

Jena frowned. "Mam is going out with the girls? What girls? This is all new to me."

Emily looked put out. "So what if I'm off for a few drinks? It makes a change. The bleeding bins go out more than me."

Jena shook her head. "See you later," she said and she left the room. The front door banged shut leaving Emily and Archie alone again. An atmosphere hung between them. Archie flicked the television on. "You'd better start getting ready then, hadn't you, if you're going out? I would hate to see the girls waiting about for you."

Emily stood up and headed for the door. "Life is for living, Archie, and, if you can't beat them, join them."

"You should be heading back to see your poorly mother, not painting the town red. Have you forgotten about the letter from your dad? Your mam is ill, might not see the rest of the year out, and you've not said a single word about it. Sad times, love. You've got your priorities all wrong."

"For your information, I have not forgotten. I'm not sure if I want to go back and see her. Those were some dark times, and she's had years to try to put it right. I've tried ringing Teresa, if you must know, but she must have changed her number. I'm planning to drive up to Burnley to see her, and get her take on it all, so quit getting on my case."

"Saying what I see, that's all. You'll regret it if anything happens to her and you haven't gone to see her. Past is past and you should move on. I'm sick of saying it to you."

Emily's eyes widened; she could feel the rage boiling up inside her. But she had too many secrets ready to spill over, so she quickly left the room before she said something she'd regret.

Chapter Ten

John had scrubbed up well – a fresh haircut, new clothes, properly dapper.

He smiled. "Thanks for the money you gave me. Once I'm back on my feet I will pay every penny back. It's embarrassing I'm sponging from you. I've always had cash about me normally. Always had enough green to treat those close to me."

"I don't want anything back, John. It was a gift and I hate to see anyone struggling – especially when you're trying to get your life straightened out."

"I would never have asked, you know."

"I know. But I know how hard it is when you get out and no one wants to give an ex-offender a chance. That's why I gave it to you. You have pride and would never have asked for help. I'd rather you have a little gift from me than go looking for dodgy earners."

He moved in closer, aware the waiter was nearby. "You won't have to do it again, love. I have chance of some good work. Big cash."

She smiled. "That's amazing! Didn't I tell you something would turn up?"

He looked shifty. "It's not that kind of work, babes." He stared at her, waiting for the penny to drop. "But it would put me back on the map, give me enough cash to find my feet and have some left over to take you on holiday, treat you right, buy you gifts."

Emily had a bad feeling. "So, what kind of work are we talking?"

He said nothing. Too many people were in earshot. Instead, he placed two fingers together, making a gun shape and looked back at her.

She felt ice in her veins. "No way, John. You've walked away from that life. You'd be a fool to be even thinking about jobs like that."

He gripped her hand in his and looked deep in her eyes. "Listen, this would be one last job. Me and you can fuck off then, live in the sun, want for nothing." He grimaced and quickly let go of her hand. "Or is this just a fling to you, a quick wham, bam, thank you mam?"

Emily shook her head. "Of course it's not. I've never done anything like this in my life. I'm risking everything even being here having a drink with you. But forget everything else, John, I just want you to be safe. And you know I can't be involved with you if that's the road you want to take."

John sat back and stared at the wall facing him. There was a silence before he spoke again. "I've fallen in love with you, Emily. I knew from the moment I laid eyes on you that you were the woman for me. Don't tell me you haven't felt the same way because you know you do. I think you want this as much as I do and, what's more, I think you've been looking for a reason to walk away from your old life. But if we're going to be together, I can't keep taking from you. As it is, you pay for everything: drinks, food, the full monty. I don't roll like that, and I want to have the money to treat you to the things I want to."

"And you can when you get a job. I'll phone around and see if I can pull any strings. But please, don't be doing anything stupid."

John bowed his head and she could tell he was in a mood. He picked up the rest of his pint and necked it in one, wiping his hand across his mouth. "Can you drop me off?"

Emily stammered. "Oh, I thought I was coming back to yours tonight? I've told Archie I'm out with the girls from work."

"Maybe you should go out with them. Maybe they're more your type of people than me."

Emily flicked the engine off when they pulled up at his house. She reached over and placed her hand on his. "John, I know I've upset you, but I care about you and want you to be safe."

"It is what it is, love. I thought we were on the same page."

"We could be but, if you tell me you are involved in an armed robbery, you can't expect me to be doing bloody cartwheels, can you?"

"I confided in you, wanted to be honest. Does that not tell you how much I care about you? No secrets. I need my woman to be OK with who I am, to understand me."

"And I do understand you, John. I'm not used to this life, I've never been in trouble with the police or anything, so don't go cold on me if I don't understand."

He said nothing, only opened the car door, and she pulled him back by his jacket. "So, what now? Are we over, are we done because of this?" She was desperate, eyes already filling with tears.

"I need time to think, Emily. Maybe you're right – I'm a criminal and you're a straight. Would anything ever work between us? We live in two different worlds."

"But we don't have to. You're a free man with a chance to start again. Please, think about it from my point of view. If anyone found out I was seeing you, I would lose my job. Doesn't it mean something how much I've already put on the line for you? Imagine if I was in the know about your criminal activity too?"

"Like I said, give me some space to get my head round everything. I'll ring you soon when I've had time to stew over a few things." The door slammed shut and he jogged towards the flats.

Emily rested her head on the steering wheel. Then she closed her eyes and banged her forehead against it. "Fuck, fuck, fuck."

Later that night, Emily lay in bed with her mobile phone clutched tightly in her hands. She had been relieved that, when she got home, Archie was already out cold, snoring on the sofa. Lying in bed, staring at her phone like a lovesick teenager, she wondered why this man had turned her world upside down. She was longing for a text, anything from John to tell her they were still together. Why, after everything he'd said tonight, was she still longing for him to say he was going to give them a chance? She heard a car door slamming outside and she got up to look. Standing back behind the blinds so nobody could see her – there was no way she was being called a plant pot by the neighbours – she tried to focus. It was Jena. Who the hell was she with? It looked like the driver was an oldish man, and they were sharing a kiss, a passionate one by the looks of things. Emily dragged her cream fluffy housecoat from the bottom of the bed and ran to the top of the stairs. The front door opened and Emily made her way down the stairs. "Who just dropped you off?"

Jena stuttered, taking her coat off slowly before she hooked it on the banister. "Mam, have you been spying on me again? I'm sick of this, honest. Stop treating me like a baby. I'm a grown woman."

"That man looked twice your age, and you were snogging the face off him like you were at a school disco. Go on, who is it?"

"None of your business, Mother, so wind your neck in and get back in bed." Jena stormed past Emily. "I'm going to bed. And, in the morning, I won't be discussing anything with anybody. End of."

Emily was back in her bed, her heart heavy. Her eyes flooded with tears and a single fat one slid down her cheek and landed on her lip. It felt like her family was falling apart – her and Archie rowing, Jena keeping secrets – and then there was John, like a ticking timebomb in the middle of everything. The sound of a text alert. She quickly wiped her eyes and reached over to the bedside cabinet for her phone. She read the message.

> You have to accept me for who I am and the risks I take. If you can't do that then what is the point of us? I wouldn't hurt anyone, and I'd be doing it for us to have a future. Have a think about it and let me know. I really care about you Emily and I hope we can sort this out. Love John xx

She read the message again, her mind doing overtime. She had feelings for him; he made her feel alive again. If there was no John, she would return to her sad life, watching TV and going to work, no one noticing her, apart from when they wanted her to cook or clean. No one else would touch her the way he did. The way this man worshipped her body made her feel powerful, desirable. The way he looked at her made her feel like she mattered. She would never find this again in her lifetime. But at what price? An affair had ripped her family apart. Yes, Jena was an adult technically, but would she ever forgive Emily if she left Archie? And for an ex-con she'd met at work? She had a lot of thinking to do, for sure. He said he wanted to do this job so he could start afresh, take her on holiday, even move in together. Was this all too much too soon, or was it what she wanted? The clock was ticking, and she had to make a choice. Emily placed her phone back on the bedside cabinet and lay staring out of the window at the silver moon shining in. Maybe now was a good time to drive over and see Teresa to talk about the letter she had received. She could get some head space and sort out her life once and for all. Her middle sister was the only person she could tell the truth to – the only one who'd been there through everything. Tomorrow was a new day.

Chapter Eleven

Teresa sat in her flat, surrounded by boxes. She had packed everything she was taking, and it seemed strange to see her home reduced to a heap of boxes. Phil, a neighbour from across the road, was helping her move. A good lad, he was, always there to help, though she'd nicknamed him Bingo Eyes. Eyes down, that was his style. He was always after getting a butcher's at her knockers. She often watched his cheeky blimps but never said anything. He was doing the move on the cheap, only charging her two hundred quid all-in. He'd always had a thing for Teresa, she knew that much, and she was always touchy-feely with the men around her. She loved that men wanted her, found her attractive. Today she was dressed in a pair of faded jeans and a white t-shirt. Of course, she had a pair of heels on too. There weren't many things Teresa couldn't do in heels. She sat down now, sipping her drink. Pink gin and lemonade was her tipple. And so what if it wasn't even twelve o'clock yet? She needed a stiff drink to help calm her nerves. She'd made sure she didn't pack the bottle as she knew she'd need a pick-me-up. All morning her stomach had been churning like a washing machine on a full spin. Ted had paid the money again – and with no funny business this time – but now she'd seen what he was capable of she was in double trouble until she was well away from this place. Teddy was a treacherous bastard, but not a psycho. He wouldn't harm her if he thought it would damage the chances of him getting his cash back. But Gavin was still on the prowl for her, and he would hurt her for the thrill of it – whether she could pay or not. So there was no way she was paying him a single penny back, she'd decided. She would rather take her chance on the run, leave her past behind and the debt she owed too. She didn't know where she was going next. Figured she'd stop off in Manchester, then who knew where next. She ran a finger around her glass and closed her eyes, thinking. She reached over to the coffee table and picked up the letter from her father. If she didn't go back now, before she ran, there would be no way they'd ever find her again. Could she go back there without bringing trouble to their door? Could she pretend it was all rosy in the garden? She wasn't sure. Maybe she would go and see Emily, try to speak to her about it. Two heads were better than one. A knocking on the door made her jump out of her skin, but she was relieved when she heard Phil shouting through her letterbox. She ran to open the door.

"Hi Phil, you know the score, love, we need to be quick. It's all those boxes piled there and I'm taking the sofa too.

The rest you can help yourself to when I'm gone. I've rented a lock-up in Manchester to store my stuff. Here is the address."

He raised his eyebrows. "So, you're really going for good then?"

"Yes, love, too much shit going on around here. Plus, my mam isn't well, and I need to be near her if it comes to the worst."

"Oh, sorry to hear that." Phil didn't really know that much about her, only what she chose to tell him. Of course, he'd seen her coming home late each evening, everyone had. The talk of the neighbourhood, she was. Fur Coat and No Knickers, they called her behind her back. She knew that, but you learned not to care. She popped her head outside the front door and, once it was clear, she turned back to Phil. "Can you be as quick as you can? Did you say your lad was helping you too?"

"Yeah, he's just shoving his shoes on. The lazy git has only just got out of bed. On my life, I don't know any man that sleeps as long as he does. I wouldn't mind, he doesn't do a tap all day and he's always knackered. Her over the road treats him like bloody Lord Fauntleroy. Irons all his clobber, cooks for him too. He says jump and she says how bloody high. I mean, I get fuck all done for me, and I'm the one out at five each morning grafting my bollocks off for them all. I need a medal, I do."

Teresa smirked. He was the same as all the men she'd ever met. That old chestnut "My wife doesn't understand me" would be next, the usual lies. She let him in the house and bolted the front door behind him, not leaving anything to chance. She was close to freedom now; she could almost taste it. Phil went into the living room and checked his wristwatch. Teresa sat fidgeting with her fingers nervously. She couldn't rest until she was gone. "You got a bargain with that motor you bought, love. A nice runner, it looks like. I didn't even know you could drive. You are always in taxis when I see you."

She chuckled. "There's plenty you don't know about me, Phil. Yes, I learned to drive when I was a lot younger. My dad taught me, in fact. He taught all my sisters. But I've not needed a car in years. Now I've got one, I can't wait to get going."

At last, they heard knocking on the door. Teresa jumped up and opened the front door. "Hi Bez, your dad's in here waiting for you."

Teresa shoved her long brown fur coat on and grabbed her handbag from the chair. "Right Phil, here's my keys to the lock-up. After you have finished, post them back through the door and the landlord can get them. I've given you the address for the lock-up, haven't I? And don't forget you take anything you want from here what's left. Get it sold and earn an extra few quid."

Phil patted his pockets and nodded. "Yep, got it. Stop worrying. Just you be careful out there. I don't want to know what's gone on, but I know it must be something bad that has made you up and leave like this. Be careful, Teresa, that's all I ask."

"You know me, Phil. I'm a survivor." She gave him a quick hug before she left. "Right, I'm here for a good time, not a long time. Take care, you two. I'm off." Her car keys jingled as she walked down the hallway. She looked back one last time before she left and, not sure if she was bidding farewell to her old house or her old life, whispered, "Goodbye."

Chapter Twelve

Shannon woke up and rubbed her knuckles into her eyes. She'd barely slept a wink. All she could hear all night long was a crying kid in the room next door. The room she was in was pretty: floral wallpaper, matching curtains and grey carpet. It was clean and simple, just a bed, wardrobe, dressing table. But right now, it felt like a palace. She pulled the duvet up and tucked it under her chin. This was the first day in a long time that she felt safe. Usually, she'd wake up next to Paddy and never knew what kind of mood he would be in. She could barely believe he was out of her life now. With any luck, he'd have been locked up after kicking off with the police. Shannon knew this was her chance – she needed to get her life in order now, stop popping pills and stop drinking. The lady she spoke to last night when she arrived at the refuge was a lovely woman. Sam was around the same age as Shannon and had told her she'd been a victim of domestic abuse too. Maybe she wasn't alone in what she was going through and being in this place could help her find her way in life again, help her fix herself. There was a soft knock on the bedroom door.

"Hello," Shannon answered. The door opened slowly, and Sam stood there smiling at her.

"Breakfast is ready, love. Do you want to come down and meet a few of the other residents?"

Shannon swallowed hard, not sure if she was ready for new faces. She had no confidence socially, not after the time she'd spent with Paddy. He'd made sure there was no socialising, no talking, just head down and keep her eyes low.

"I'll get ready and come down in a few minutes, if that's alright?"

"Of course it is. Take all the time in the world. Just to let you know that everyone here is here for the same reasons as you so you'll be among friends, people who understand how it feels to be where you are now."

Shannon smiled softly and nodded. "Thanks Sam, I'll be down soon."

"Oh, I sorted you some clothes out and put them in your wardrobe last night. I know you didn't come with a lot of personal belongings, so they are yours if you want them."

Sam closed the door behind her, and Shannon was alone again. She missed Frank with an ache inside – but the refuge team had told her the foster home they'd had to drop him at would treat him like a king. She hoped he wasn't pining for her like he was pining for him. It was another reason to get herself straightened out – clean up so she could get her own little place with room for Frank too. With effort she pulled herself from the bed and walked to the white double wardrobe. As she opened it, she could see a rail full of t-shirts and blouses and underneath them on a shelf were jeans and shoes. She slowly examined the items of clothing. These were lovely, better than anything she'd ever owned. She picked out a bright green top and a pair of jeans. Sam had worked out her size perfectly. Once she was ready, she stood at the full-length mirror and studied herself. She'd hated to really look at herself for so long, it felt like a stranger in the mirror. Was this really her? She wasn't sure. She walked slowly towards her reflection and stared for a few more seconds. Her eyes flooded with tears and her legs buckled underneath her. She sat on the floor with her legs pulled up tightly to her chest. She needed this, she needed to get it all out, all the misery she'd suffered, the abuse both mentally and physically, it was all coming to the surface now.

Shannon walked into the dining area and kept her eyes down, still not ready to talk to people. She pulled out a chair at the table and sat next to a woman who looked a similar age to her. "Help yourself to a cuppa, and grab some toast." The woman introduced herself as Natalie. "Did you come here late last night? I heard the door opening and closing, and that usually means we have a new resident."

"Yes, it was after midnight when I got here. How long have you been here?"

Natalie munched her toast and spoke with her mouth full. "Three weeks. I'm so grateful to all the staff here, they do a brilliant job. Honest, I was in a really bad place with my fella and, if I hadn't got out when I did, he would have done something serious to me, probably killed me."

"Yeah, same as, Natalie." After all the years of denying it, hiding her scars, pretending everything was OK, it felt surreal to say it out loud, and to a virtual stranger. But it felt good. She'd imagined she'd feel embarrassed, like she'd let it happen, but instead she felt like she was getting her voice back, finally telling the truth. "My man was a bloody head-the-ball too. He wouldn't let me leave the house, kicked ten bags of shit out of me whenever he felt like it, arsehole."

"The thing to remember is that you are safe now. The girls here are trying to find me my own place so I can start again. They have spoken with the police and I have a restraining order already served on the idiot who I was with. That means, if he comes anywhere near me, he'll be arrested and locked up."

Shannon wanted to know more. "So, if he comes anywhere near you, you just ring the police and he will be arrested?"

"Yep, they are trying to get me a panic button too for when I'm in my own house. It's kind of like a necklace that I wear around my neck with a button on. Any sign of danger, I press it and the police will be with me in seconds."

Shannon grabbed a piece of toast. "Well, I guess I'll be needing one of them too, because Paddy has always warned me that, if I ever leave him,he will come and find me."

Natalie rolled her eyes and sighed. "Yep, my guy said exactly the same thing to me. I suppose that's why I stayed as long as I did. I thought I'd never get away from him. You'll find most of the girls here say the same."

Shannon slurped her cup of tea and began to relax. "So, how many other ladies are here?"

"Six. There was seven but Gemma got off a few days ago and went back to her husband. Said she wanted to try again with him, missed him. On my life, she was black and blue when she came here one night. He'd gone to town on her and she's lucky there was no lasting damage."

"What, she went back to a man who'd been hitting her?" Shannon couldn't imagine ever giving Paddy a second look, never mind a second chance.

Natalie sat back and folded her arms. "It happens a lot. Some women just can't hack life on their own – they've been brainwashed into believing they need their abusers. Sick."

"Well, I won't ever be going back to Paddy, let me tell you. He's a prick, a drunken prick at that."

Natalie started laughing and picked up her cigarettes from the table. "That's what I like to hear. Fancy a fag, we have to go outside in the garden to smoke. That's where I spend most of my day, if I'm being honest."

Shannon was gagging for a smoke and stood up to follow Natalie. She had one hundred and one questions to ask her. Both women sat on chairs in the garden and lit up. "I don't have a pot to piss in, Natalie. Paddy had my bank card and all my benefits went into that account."

"The team here will help sort out all your benefits and that. They can even help get you grants to furnish your new home. Where is it you are wanting to go?"

Shannon sucked hard on her ciggie and blew a large cloud of grey smoke from her mouth. "I want to go back home, near my mam and dad. They live round Moston. I've not seen them for years, though. I wonder if they'd even recognise me."

"Yes, that's what happens. They isolate you and make you think you have nobody but them. It's good that you have family, somebody who cares about you."

Shannon's eyes clouded. "I don't know about that. We all fell out over some pretty nasty stuff, and since then we've drifted away from each other. I used to talk to my sisters every now and then but I've lost contact with them since, well, since Paddy locked me up."

"So, get back in touch with everyone. You need your family around you when you're going through crap in your life. I wish I had family who I could turn to."

Shannon could see a tear forming in the corner of Natalie's eye. She patted her arm softly. "Do you not have any close family?"

Natalie choked back the tears and took a few seconds to speak. "No, they disowned me when they found out I was seeing a black guy, told me never to darken their door again. It was my dad more than my mam. He was racist, plain and simple. Tyrone said he would come and meet my parents when I first started seeing him, but I always put it off. I knew in my heart my dad would never let him over the front door step. I confided in my mother, showed her a photograph of me and Tyrone together when she asked to have a look at my new man, and I'll never forget that look in her eye when she seen him for the first time. She was gobsmacked, handed me my phone back like it held some sort of disease. She couldn't hide how she felt. I could see it in her eyes."

"That's terrible. How can they be like that in this day and age?"

"Yeah, I know. Anyway, Tyrone was out with me in a pub not far from where we lived, when I spotted one of my dad's mates. He marched over and gave us both a mouthful of abuse. I can't even repeat what he said to Tyrone. And, as you can guess, the rest is history. He went straight to our house and bubbled me to my dad." Shannon sat chewing on her fingernail as Natalie continued. "I'll never forget the look in my dad's eyes when he told me I was dead to him. He couldn't even look at me. Spat at me, he did. Told me to get my stuff together and get out of his house. My mam just stood by his side and never said a word. I'll never forgive her for that, not now, not ever. But, anyway, that was when I was a young girl. I broke up with Tyrone after about six months and I never went back home. So when I met my ex – the bastard who's been beating me – I had nowhere else to go. I'd rather be six feet under than go back to my folks. Being alone isn't always great but it's better than being around people you hate."

They finished their smokes and went back indoors.

Sam was waiting for her. "I've been looking for you. Can we have a quick chat?" She walked through the double doors and led Shannon inside a small office. She sat down behind her desk and started clicking the keypad on her laptop. "So, first things first. Are you getting any benefits?" Shannon sat on the wooden chair facing Sam. "I was, but Paddy has my bank card and to tell you the truth I don't even know how much I get. He handled all my money."

Sam gave her a sympathetic look. "Well, not anymore. You will have your own money to look after yourself." She took a few details from Shannon and told her she was contacting the benefits agency to update them. Once she'd finished inputting all the new information, she sat back in her chair. "The police have been in touch with me. They want to come and take a statement from you. Paddy is in custody for assaulting a police officer and it looks like they will be keeping him locked away until he goes to court."

Shannon panicked. "I'm not going to court. I couldn't face him. I never want to see him again. Can I not just walk away and start my life over? Why do they need a statement from me? I've already told them what was happening, and that should be enough."

"I know how hard this is for you, Shannon, but we have to make sure you will be safe in the future. We can apply for a restraining order once you have given the police a statement. A lot of the women who come here feel the way you do about going to court, but it's the only way legally that we can help and make sure he never steps foot near you again."

Shannon felt hot and flustered as she stuttered, "But that's being a grass. Snitches get stitches and all that. I'm away from him now. I just want some peace. To live my life."

Sam could tell Shannon was ready to break down and didn't want to push her any further. Time was a good healer and maybe in a few days she would feel differently. She changed the subject. "I see you have met Natalie. She's a lovely lady and she'll show you the ropes. The rest of the ladies should be down later."

"How long can I stay here? Natalie was talking about getting her own place, but I want to stay still and sort my head out."

Sam looked at her notes and scribbled something down. "You can stay here until the local authorities find you somewhere safe to stay, hopefully out of the area."

"I want to go to Moston, be back near my family. Will they be able to send me there?"

"We can do our best. For now, let's concentrate on getting you stronger."

Shannon scratched her bony wrists. She always scratched at her body when she was anxious. "Can I use the phone to ring my dad?"

Sam looked apprehensive. Making calls to people from this safe house was a dangerous business and could put all her residents at risk. They had policies and procedures to follow. "Yes, but you cannot tell him where you are. And I have to be with you while you make the call."

"That's fine. But why can't I tell him where I am?"

"Telling anyone where you are leaves us all open. One of the ladies done that once before and told her ex where she was staying. He came up here, smashed all our windows, damaged all our cars and said he wasn't moving until we called the police."

"I get you. If Paddy got wind of where I was, he would be the same. The man is loopy, a couple of butties short of a picnic."

"Don't think you're going through any of this alone, Shannon. We have a counsellor on site today if you would like to go and see her. She helps a lot of our ladies and understands what you're facing now, adjusting to life after abuse. Also, we have a yoga class in about an hour, if you fancy that?"

Shannon smiled. "I think I'm just going to rest today, if that's OK? I don't think I'm ready for counselling or yoga yet. But Sam, I mean it when I say thanks for all your help. You do an amazing job here for all the ladies. Without places like this, a lot of us wouldn't live to tell the tale."

Sam explained that her own mother had been a victim of domestic abuse and she knew how much it could affect a person. She was only a child when she witnessed it, but she still held the memories, still had the nightmares of watching her mother getting beaten. "So what I do is more than a job to me. It's about giving people their lives back. If you want to make the call, you can do it now."

"That would be great. Only can you give me a moment to get my head together? I've not spoken to them for a long time, and I need to practise in my head what I'm going to say. Don't worry, I won't tell them anything about where I am or what has happened."

Sam started to catch up on some paperwork. "Give me a shout when you're ready," she said.

Shannon sat in her seat, ragging her fingers through her hair. How would she start the conversation, what would she say? What if Teresa and Emily were already there and she was the only one missing? The one they would say only ever cared about herself. There were a lot of things they needed to talk about – more than she could imagine saying out loud. But you had to start somewhere. She bit down on her bottom lip and lifted her head. "I'm ready, Sam."

Sam asked for the number she was calling and made sure she pressed one-four-one before she dialled it, so nobody could trace the call. She passed the phone over to Shannon.

With every ring, Shannon's mouth got drier. "Hello, Dad, is that you? It's Shannon," she said anxiously. She listened to the voice down the line and pushed the phone closer to her ear, tears already forming. "Yes, I got the letter and I'm doing my best to get home. I'll have some money soon and, once I've got it, I will be there. Are either of the others there yet?" She cringed as she said this, half expecting the phone to be dragged from her father's hand and for the next voice she heard to be one of her sisters telling her what a waste of space she was. "What, none of them have been in touch? I thought our Emily would have been there straight away. I know stuff has happened, Dad, but we have to get over that now and stand together as one."

The conversation went on for at least ten more minutes and, by the end of it, Shannon was crying her eyes out. Maybe she had only followed the others when they said they wanted nothing more to do with their parents. In their fury at their mum, none of them had really thought about their dad, had they? He had been hurting too when they all jumped ship and never returned.

Shannon lay in her bed and stared out at the night sky. What a bloody disaster this was. Her so-called family, her life: it was one fucked-up mess. The first thing in the morning she was going to sit down with Sam and ask if she could go home to visit her parents, explain that her mother was ill and these could be her final months. Sooner or later, she knew Emily and Teresa would turn up there, and what then? She could see them both now, whispering behind her back, pointing the finger at her, calling her names. She dragged the duvet up and tucked it over her shoulders. She needed the oblivion of sleep if she was going to go back home and sort her life out. She closed her eyes slowly, but opened them again straight away. Paddy's image was right there behind her eyes, staring back at her, growling, showing his teeth. If he couldn't get to her in her waking life, he was still going to haunt her dreams. His words rang in her ears: "I'll find you no matter where you are." Quickly she searched her pockets for her tablets. She'd take two tonight, maybe three. She swigged cold water from the glass and popped her pills. She'd start getting clean tomorrow, but tonight was going to be a long one, for sure. Paddy was lying heavy on her mind, and she was going to need all the help she could get to banish him from her mind and get any kind of rest. But she'd better get used to it, she told herself. She would have to sleep with one eye open every night. Never let her guard down. Not now, not ever.

Chapter Thirteen

Emily drove along the motorway with the radio on quietly. What a miserable day it was. Big grey clouds hung low in the sky. She'd told Archie she was going to see Teresa and he seemed glad she was going to sort things out at last. She stared at the line of traffic ahead and sighed. She was going away for her own reasons, too: to clear her head, to decide if she could be with John still, be in love with a criminal. Teresa would listen to her, give her good advice. After all, she'd been there for her in the past when she was going through hard times. Times when she'd fucked up big time, times when she had nowhere else to turn for comfort. She checked her mobile phone again. No messages, no missed calls. John had left the ball in her court, and she had to be sure about all of this before she replied to him. Half of her wanted to ring him and say she would do anything so they could be together, but the sensible side of her dragged her back and spelled out all the problems that could arise if she was in a relationship with a known criminal. And there was Archie and Jena to think about. Emily could deal with Archie – this whole thing had made her question her marriage again and acknowledge that she'd been lying to herself when she said she'd forgiven Archie for his affair. But Jena? How could she tell Jena to be careful of who she was dating when she was losing her own head over an armed robber struggling to quit the business? She had so many scenarios going around in her head and she couldn't wait to share them with her sister. Teresa had been totally open about having affairs with married men in the past. She never let anything get in the way of what – or who – she wanted.

Emily's phone started ringing and Archie's name flashed on the screen. She quickly reached over and put it on silent. If she spoke to him now, she would probably tell him they were over and she wanted him gone from the house before she returned home. Instead, she turned Smooth FM up and sang along with Whitney Houston. Emily loved a power ballad and when she was cleaning, she always had her playlist on speaker. Jena called it a load of old shit and complained it was too loud, but Emily ignored her and sang around the house as she cleaned up.

Archie and Emily had shared all that in the past, laughing and singing along at concerts. They were the good old days when love was young and pure. Archie was a right looker back in his day and he had the gift of the gab. Emily always said that was one of the things that attracted her to him in the first place. He had made her laugh, made her feel confident about herself. Archie would kiss her anywhere. He didn't care if they were in public, or if people could see them. He would shout out at the top of his voice how much he loved Emily and didn't care who heard him.

Emily's heart sank as she thought about the good old days. Her husband had been her soul mate, her best friend. But he had to go and spoil it. Why wasn't she enough for him? She'd asked herself that hundreds of times and always came back to the same answer. She'd asked Archie why he'd been unfaithful and he could never explain it, but she knew the reason. They'd got married young and expected a baby to come along straight away. And when one didn't, they'd both changed. He said the affair was a mistake, a one-night thing, no explanation, no nothing. For weeks after the affair was uncovered, she took to her bed. It was Teresa who finally made her get out of bed, dragged her out, she did. Emily could remember it like yesterday.

"Get that arse up out of bed. How dare you crumble because of a man? Get over here and look at yourself in the mirror." She'd pulled Emily out of bed and made her stand tall in front of the silver bedroom mirror. "Look at what you've become. If someone knocks you down, you get back up, girl, even stronger than you was before. Go out and sleep with ten men. Show that weasel of a husband what you are about, what makes you ill, makes you better. Trust me, I know."

Emily was thankful for that day. Without it, maybe she would have still been there wallowing in her own self-pity. Teresa booked her in the hairdressers that same day and made her traipse around town to get some new outfits.

In all fairness, the tough love approach worked, because after that she was back on her feet. It took months before she could even look at her husband again. Teresa said she wanted to one-bomb him every time she looked at him. But Emily had been a woman on a mission. When they were out in public you would never have thought they had problems. To the untrained eye, they were loving, always together, the perfect couple. It couldn't have been further from the truth. But then Jena came along, and it all seemed to get brushed under the carpet in the chaos of raising a baby.

Emily came off the motorway now and let out a laboured breath. Forty minutes she'd been stuck on it, and she'd scranned half a bag of chocolate limes through boredom. She headed onto the main road and familiar landmarks started to pop out at her. There was the Hat and Feathers. She'd had many a good night with her sister in that boozer. They'd rolled out of there in the early hours, laughing and singing. Teresa always knew how to make sure they had a good night out.

Emily pulled up outside Teresa's house. She spotted immediately that the front door was open slightly. She shook her head. Teresa was a right empty-head sometimes. She'd probably been rushing in and forgot to close it. Emily turned the engine off and got out of the car. She walked up the garden path and edged in through the door.

"Hello, Teresa, it's me, Emily. Are you home?"

She stood in the hallway now. There were voices in the other room and it suddenly struck her that Teresa might have a man in there with her. She always seemed to have some bloke on the go. Her cheeks flushed just thinking about it. She paused, then gently knocked on the living room door.

"Hello," she whispered. The door swung open and there was a bloke, dripping in sweat, heaving boxes. He looked Emily up and down and quickly wiped his forehead with his sleeve.

"Oh, morning lovely. Who you after?"

"Teresa. I'm her sister."

He started dismantling a wooden table. "I'm her neighbour, Phil. Did she know you were coming? Because she left about an hour ago. Didn't mention any visitors."

Emily entered the room. "What time did she say she was coming back?"

"She won't be coming back here, love. She's done one, moved away."

"What, for good?"

Phil stopped what he was doing to explain. "Teresa has had a bit of bother with some geezer. As far as I know, he's a bit of a meat-head and she's not sticking around to see what happens. I've seen him here a few times, lurking on the street waiting for her to come home. On my life, he gave me the creeps, so God knows how your sister felt. A big man, always has a couple of cronies with him."

Emily felt like she'd had the wind knocked out of her. All the journey, she'd been thinking about getting Teresa's help, little thinking her sister might be the one who really needed help.

Phil could see she was upset. "Tell you what, I'll pop the kettle on and make you a quick cuppa. I'm due a break."

Phil left the room, and suddenly there was loud banging in the hallway. Moments later, the living room door was booted open, and a man stood there. "Where the fuck is she? Don't fucking lie to me because I'll fuck you both up. That bitch owes me money and I want every fucking penny back."

Emily went cold. Phil's legs buckled and he had to steady himself on the door frame. "Listen mate, I'm here to clear the house. I know nothing only she said she was going back home to Manchester."

Emily glared at him. What a gobshite he was. And he was still talking.

"This is her sister. She'll know more than me."

Gavin ran at her, dragging her up by the back of her collar and pinning her against the wall. "So, bitch, start talking. Ring her. Tell her to get her arse back here, because you're going nowhere until she does."

Phil zipped up his black sports jacket. "I'll be getting off then. I can finish off later," he stuttered.

The two men who'd come in with Gavin stepped in front of Phil and eyeballed him. "Sit the fuck down, little man. You're going nowhere either."

Phil swallowed hard, his mouth drying up. "Come on lads, I've told you, I'm only here to shift a few things. I'm nothing to do with this. I just want to get my stuff and go."

Gavin roared, "Don't make me repeat myself. Sit the fuck down before I chin you."

Emily went into her bag and quickly, covertly, sent a message while this commotion was going on, her fingers trembling with every word she texted. Gavin was back at her side now, his eyes dancing with madness. "Do you have a number for your sister?"

"I do, but I've tried it a few times and it's not connecting. She must have got a new phone."

"Bullshit. Show me."

Emily pulled her phone out of her bag. She saw a call from John flashing. Gavin snatched the phone from her hand and stared at the call until it stopped ringing. Emily was sweating, her palms hot and clammy. She met Gavin's eyes and quickly looked away.

Gavin changed his tone. "We can do this the easy way or the hard way, love. Your sister owes me money and I want it back. Ten grand, the slapper owes me, and she's been dodging me for months."

"Why does she owe you money?"

"Don't play the innocent with me," Gavin scoffed. Then he paused. "You do know your sister is a brass, an escort? Banks don't exactly love giving loans to hookers."

Emily screwed her face up. "A brass? Is she hell! She works in a care home, she's a manager."

Gavin and his boys laughed. "A fucking care home? Are you having a laugh, or what? She looks after a few old uns alright, but not in the way you think."

Emily had her back up and, even though these men could have ended her life right there and then, she was still sticking up for her sister, convinced they had got this wrong. You heard about these cases of mistaken identity all the time. "I would know if my sister was selling her body. For as long as I can remember, she has worked at Oak Bank nursing home. I've picked her up from there before now."

Gavin chuckled. "She's been a prossy for as long as I can remember. Clearly, she's not a bad actress either. Fooled you, anyway. Why do you think I got rid of her? She's a lying bitch. But I'll give her that, she had me over big time. I gave her the money to help her out and she promised me it would be back to me within a few months. She's a slapper who wouldn't know the truth if it bit her on the arse."

Emily could feel the doubt trickling in. She had wondered where all that money had come from in the past – she'd assumed Teresa had rich fellas, but it sounded like she'd got mixed up with the wrong guy when she found Gavin. "Did she pay any of the money back?"

"At first, she was bunging me money all the time, but that soon stopped, and that's when she started hiding from me. I'm not going to lie, I had a bit of a soft spot for your sister and hated seeing her struggle, but, come on, she's a piss-taker. Doesn't she know my reputation?" Gavin seemed to be lost in the moment and didn't speak for a couple of seconds. Then he gripped Emily again and got nose-to-nose with her. "So, let me tell you something for nothing. If you can't clear your sister's debt, you're staying with me until she fucking pays every penny back."

Phil chirped in again. "And me?"

Emily could see by Gavin's reaction that he wanted to one-arrow him and shut him up. The man at Phil's side had had enough of hearing his voice, too, and backhanded him. "You shut the fuck up and say nothing."

Phil's head went west and Emily could see a red hand mark appearing on his face.

She felt adrenaline surging through her. "Serves you right, bloody coward."

Gavin was back at Emily now. He lifted her bag from the floor and looked inside her purse. He pulled out two bank cards. "You must have some cash – how about a down-payment?"

Emily tried to remain calm. She was used to dealing with offenders of all stripes – except usually their crimes were in the past. She kept her poker face. "I've got a couple of hundred pounds in my account and that's it."

Gavin held the cards out to one of his men. "Wes, go to the bank and see if this bint is lying, or what." He turned back to Emily and spoke through gritted teeth. "Pin number. Don't fuck about with me because, if he goes to the bank and you're lying, I'll pull every one of your bastard teeth out. So be wise, woman, and think about this."

Emily's mask slipped and she started crying; this was all too much for her. Her life was quiet and peaceful, not this. Was this karma for crossing the line with John? Suddenly her old simple life didn't seem so dull. "One, nine, two, one. It's all my savings. I've worked hard for that money. You can't take that."

Gavin squeezed his fat fingers around her throat and went in her face again. "And, what? You don't think I work hard for my money? I'm taking everything you have, just like your sister did with me. Do you think she gives a shit about having me over?"

"I'm nothing to do with this. Teresa is the one who owes you money, not me. I want to find her just as much as you do."

Gavin dipped his hand into her handbag again and pulled out her driving licence. "Wes, you take her to the bank and make sure both accounts are emptied."

Wes patted his inside pocket and slowly pulled out a silver pistol. He pointed it at her. "Any fucking about and I'll end you. You heard what Gav said, empty each account. I'll be right behind you, so any funny business and you will be over, do you get me?"

Phil looked like he was having a nervous breakdown. He dropped his head into his hands with a look of despair. He whispered to her, "Do what they ask. The sooner this is over the better."

Emily's legs were like jelly when Gavin released his grip on her. She felt like she was going to pass out. Maybe looking up her family hadn't been her best idea. Sometimes the past was better undisturbed. She followed Wes out of the door, her heart in her mouth. She'd seen the gun, knew, if she tried to get away, the heavy would shoot her dead. She knew some people carried guns for show – but these guys meant it, she could tell.

She got into the back of the car, sobbing her eyes out. "This is my savings, it's all I have. I've worked day in day out to make this – ten thousand pounds that I've been saving to buy a new car."

The engine flicked over and Wes pulled onto the street. Her words fell on deaf ears. Emily tried again. "Please, let me go. This is my sister's problem, not mine. Let me go and I'll never tell anyone what happened here?"

The driver glanced at her through the rear-view mirror. He looked evil. "I thought you said you had a couple of hundred quid. You're like your sister, you are – a fucking liar."

Emily's body was shaking from head to toe. She thought she'd outrun the worst day of her life – but today was definitely a contender.

As she got back into the car she was still shaking. She'd hoped the bank cashier would have noticed and stopped the withdrawal, but she'd simply gone through the motions, peered at her ID and asked a couple of security questions. The envelope of cash looked pitifully small to think that was her life savings. Wes snatched the money from her and wasted no time spinning off. The ride back to the house seemed to take forever and, as she watched the driver nervously, she contemplated what she could do. She could grab him from behind, choke him maybe. But he was stronger than she was and what then, when he broke free? He would end her just like he'd told her he would. She was helpless.

Gavin smiled when Wes pushed Emily back through the living room door. He passed the money over to the main man. "Over ten big uns there, our kid."

Phil gasped a sigh of relief, feeling sure this would have bought his release. Surely these idiots would go now, and he could go back to his normal life.

Gavin nodded. At last, the debt was paid. He stood up, looking like the cat who'd got the cream. "Nice doing business with you. Tell your sister thank you, too."

Emily wanted to run at him and scratch his eyes out but knew better. She sat staring at the floor. The three men left the room and Phil was about to stand up when there was a commotion in the hallway. He ran over to Emily and hid behind her. "What the hell is happening now?"

Emily pushed Phil away from her with both hands. She looked around the room and grabbed a heavy metal ornament. There was no way she was taking this sitting down anymore. She would fight for her life if it came to it. Phil followed suit and took up the sweeping brush. Like that would do any damage. They listened to shouting, screaming, banging in the hallway. Neither of them dared move. Perhaps Wes had turned on Gavin hoping for a better cut? Finally, the living room door swung open, and she saw Gavin coming back into the room. But someone was behind him.

"John," she gasped.

Gavin was pushed to the back wall as John pointed a gun at him. "You fucking move an inch and I'll send you to meet your maker."

Over Phil's shoulder, Emily could see Wes laid on the hallway floor, not moving, blood trickling down his head.

The other guy must have run off. Phil seemed to sense his chance, because he sprinted to the door and turned back quickly before he left. "I'm out of here. I never seen a thing."

Emily ran to John and hugged him. "He took my money, made me go to the bank and draw it all out."

"I've got your money here, love, don't you worry about anything. You go outside and get in the car, I'll be out in a minute after I've dealt with this wanker."

Gavin stood with his back against the wall. The tide had turned and now he was the one trying to talk his way out of danger. He shouted at John, "Do yourself a favour and fuck off before you do something you'll seriously regret. The rest of my boys will be on the way and, no matter where you are, they will find you and end your fucking life. Walk away, lad. Do what's right."

John gently pushed Emily. "Go, start the car up. You don't need to see or hear this."

She ran out of the room but stopped to look down at Wes. She covered her mouth with both hands: he wasn't moving. This was all too much for her. She couldn't take it in.

Emily started her car up, hands still shaking, and kept looking over at the house, waiting for John to come out. "Please, don't do anything silly, John, just get out of there safe," she muttered. Every ounce of her body was filled with fear.

The rear door swung open, and John dived in. "Drive, quick, get the fuck away from here."

Emily sped out onto the open road, nearly ploughing into a black Astra.

"Whoa, keep your eyes on the road," John screamed. "Pull over and I'll drive," he shouted.

Emily was a bag of nerves. She pulled over, but still clung to the steering wheel like it was a lifebuoy. "My God, what on Earth has just happened? I only went to see my sister and look at me. I can't believe what Teresa's got herself mixed up in – they weren't messing. They told me they would kill me. I'm so glad you got my message. I dread to think what would have happened if you hadn't come. But how did you get here so quickly?"

John gave her a gentle push. "Pure blind luck. I was in Accrington at a mate's. I got him to drop me off, but I wasn't expecting the full heavy mob. Come on, swap seats. We need to get away from here."

Emily opened the car door and ran round to the passenger side. She got in next to him, and spotted the bright red blood on his hands. She clipped her seat belt in, not daring to say a word until they were on the motorway.

"John, please tell me you didn't shoot him."

He kept his eyes on the road and spoke calmly. "Nah, I just give him a good arse-kicking. He's not worth a bullet."

"But what'll happen now? He'll come looking for you, he said he would, you heard him."

"Stop worrying. I've met his sort a hundred times before. We all piss in the same pot in this game, love, and he'll take this on the chin if he knows what's good for him."

"I'm so sorry for involving you, John. I should have called the police."

"Hush, woman. Do you think the police would have got to you in time? I doubt it."

"But the guy in the hallway, is he dead? He wasn't moving when I passed him."

"He'll move when he comes round. He only got a belt over his head, though I could have gone to town on him."

"John, I'm so scared."

"Sssh, we can go to mine and chill for a bit. What the hell happened, anyway? I thought you were Little Miss Straight?"

"I was going to stay with my sister for a few days, sort my head out. When I got there, there was a guy clearing all her stuff away. Said she'd left and was moving back near her family. I was only there a short time when that crank showed up and started terrorising me."

John nodded, checking in the rear-view mirror that nobody was following them. "It's the world we live in, Em. Bad people about, wherever you are."

"You might as well know the full story. He said Teresa is an escort, a brass. Said she had borrowed ten thousand pounds from him."

"And is she?"

Emily looked down. "I thought she worked in a care home, but thinking about it, over the years she was always on holidays for weeks, nice designer clothes, handbags. But she has a good salary. She's a manager."

"Only your sister knows the truth, but if she's dealing with loan sharks and not paying them back, then she's asking for trouble. My mate's Mrs only borrowed five hundred quid from a loan man, and when she couldn't pay he cleared the house while she was out, took the TV, took the kids' PlayStation, left the place wrecked. Like I said, a dangerous world."

"I need to phone home as soon as. Tell Archie that Teresa isn't here. I'll tell him I'll stay in a hotel tonight."

John squirmed as she mentioned her husband's name. He tapped his fingers rapidly on the steering wheel. "So, why didn't you ring me before today, Emily? I told you to think about what you wanted. You know – us…"

She shifted in her seat. "I was having some head space. Going to see Teresa was so I could think properly."

"You was binning me off, then?"

"No, I never said that. It's a big decision. If we were to be a proper couple, it would mean goodbye to everything I've ever known. It's a lot to risk when we've only known each other such a short time."

"Long time or short time, I knew from the moment I saw you. And it's time for you to make up your mind. So, do I drop you at home or at mine? No point in you coming back with me now if you don't want to be with me. I've put all my cards on the table, Emily. I've been honest with you. And, as you've just seen, I'd do anything for you. That guy back there was a fucking idiot and I didn't care who he was or what he could do to me. I only wanted to save you and make you safe."

She touched his warm hand. "Take me to your house, John. I don't need any more time to think. I want you and everything that goes with you. You're right – you risked everything for me and I'm willing to do the same for you."

John smiled from cheek to cheek and nodded. "I'm glad. Just one other thing left now – you need to tell your husband about us. I don't like sharing, Em, and I know me and my head. I'll go mental if I know you are going back to your husband every night."

She panicked. "John, I'll do it – but I've got to do it right. I need time to sort my home life out. It's not that simple. I have a daughter, you know that, and a job, a mortgage, lots of things I can't simply walk away from."

"I'm not saying like right away, I'm just saying sooner rather than later."

Emily nodded. It was only right she should tell her husband that she had met somebody else. It would be hard, but it was something she would have to do. Lying never made a bad situation better. She wondered if she'd be able to keep the family home, or whether they'd have to sell and split the money. Where would Jena live? She knew once she'd set the ball rolling, there would be no way back. Emily pulled her mobile phone out of her bag and switched the silent mode off. As soon as she did, her phone started ringing. It was Archie. She showed it to John.

"Answer it, then," he said.

Her fingers fumbled as she answered the call. How embarrassing was this to speak to her husband in front of her lover?

"Hello," she said in a timid voice.

Archie was talking fast, and she found it hard to understand him.

"What, Teresa is *there*?" Emily was baffled.

He carried on talking and she cut him short. "Please put Teresa on the phone, Archie."

John was saying nothing. He kept his eyes on the road, but she knew he was listening to every word she was saying. "Teresa, you're not on speaker, are you? Good. Don't say a word to Archie, but you need to come and meet me. I went to your house this morning. Some nutcase called Gavin was there. It was bad, Teresa, really bad. Yes, I'm fine now. I'll explain what happened when I see you. It sounds like you've got some stuff to tell me, too." She listened carefully to every word her sister was saying back to her. "No, I'm not hurt, thank God. Tell Archie I'm staying in a hotel near your house and you are driving back to join me. Tell him we are going to a spa or something – a girls' trip. You know how to lie, so make something up. Text me your new number and I'll tell you where to meet me." She ended the call there. There was no way she wanted Archie back on the line asking a hundred and one questions. He would have had her there all day.

Emily could sense John was more subdued than he'd been before. "I love you, John. I know I've never said it before, but I do. A life without you is not worth thinking about. You make me feel alive again, but today you literally saved my life."

"I love you, too. We will be sorted once you've told your fella about us. I know it's hard, but I am not into sneaking about with someone's Mrs."

"I know, I know, I'll sort it." Emily dropped her head back onto the head rest and closed her eyes. She was mentally and physically drained. But she'd talk it all through with Teresa – some secrets were too big for one person.

Chapter Fourteen

Teresa pulled up in the car park, feeling edgy. It was pitch-black outside and only one streetlamp sprayed yellow light on where she had parked. At last, she could see someone walking towards her. Her eyes widened – she was still thinking about being attacked by Teddy's thug the other day. She sat forward and peered through the windscreen. Phew, about bloody time. The car door opened, and Emily jumped into the passenger side. From the moment she locked eyes with her sister, Emily burst out crying and hugged her. There was no way she was letting go, either.

"Oh my God, I've missed you so much. Upon my life, I've missed you."

Teresa, too, shed a tear. She was a tough cookie but at times like this her emotions got too much for her. She pulled back a little and held her sister's hands. "Emily, what on Earth has happened?"

Emily rolled her shoulders back and told her sister everything that had gone on at the house. As she got to the end of the story, Teresa had her head in her hands. "I'm so sorry, so, so, sorry. This was my problem – I was dealing with it. I never meant anyone else to get caught up in it. If it wasn't for that bloke you called, you could be dead. Who is this John who came to help you? You need to tell me so I can say thank you from the bottom of my heart. I tell you what, this is a wake-up call – me and my life need sorting out big time."

Emily had been so busy going through the events of the morning she hadn't had time to ask Teresa the truth about whether she really was an escort and, now there was time to ask, she realised she wanted more than anything to share her own secret before she dived into anyone else's. Her voice was low, head bowed. "John's the man I've been seeing. I met him at work. I can't believe it myself, but we are madly in love and want to be together. I didn't know who else to message who'd be any use in a situation like that."

Teresa looked surprised. "Are you having a laugh? You've got what most women want – a good fella, nice family, nice home. Don't jeopardise it all for some fling. Not that I'm telling you not to have your fun. Fuck him and get it out of your system. You never ever, leave your husband for a bit of a leg-over. First rule in the game."

Emily was shocked. "It's not a fling, we're in love."

"Love's all well and good, but what will you have when the lust wears off? I get you might be bored in your marriage, but do what every other woman does when the marriage is stale and have a quick knee-trembler. Trust me, it works. And can he look after you like Archie has done for all these years? You say you met at work – are you in the same office?"

Emily was sheepish. "He doesn't work at the moment," she stuttered. "Look, if you must know, he's an ex-convict, one of my clients, not a colleague." There you go, she'd said it, told that truth for the first time.

Teresa was up in arms, holding nothing back. "Oh, this gets worst by the bleeding minute. Are you right in the head? An ex-con, for crying out loud. Give your head a shake, woman, and smell the coffee."

Emily was fuming, and her rage shook down the other questions she'd be holding on to. "Go on then, answer this, if you're so wise about relationships – are you a brass?"

The question took Teresa by surprise. She took a few seconds to digest said it, then retaliated. "No, am I hell. What makes you say that?"

"Gavin told me. Said you'd been at it for years. Don't lie to me, not after what I've been through on your account today. If that's what you work as, then be honest with me."

Teresa had never been ashamed of her choices, but she also didn't think they were anyone else's business and, if this had been anybody other than her own flesh and blood, she would have told them to go and take a running jump. She stared out at the moonlight and a lump rose in her throat. "Yes, it's the truth. I've done what I had to do to get by. You know me, I could never work a nine-to-five job for peanuts. I've always wanted more, always wanted to have the best of everything."

Emily snapped, "And selling your body was the only thing you could have thought of to earn money?"

Teresa sagged, hurt by her sister's words. "I only started doing it to get a bit of money. A few of my friends were doing it. I never had sex with them at first. No, I just went to functions with them. But if I wanted more, so did the guys. And yes, it turned out I was good at it. But I'll not lie – these last few years, times have been hard."

There was a silence between them. Teresa sparked up a cigarette and passed one to Emily. "We're a mess, aren't we? I was coming to your house today to sort my life out. To build bridges, maybe even go and see our mam. I want to have a peaceful life. I'm getting too old for all this shit. Did you get a letter, too?"

Emily nodded. "But I didn't know what to do. I thought talking it over with you might clear my head – turns out it blew everything up. Neither of us are the women we've pretended to be, I guess."

Teresa stroked a finger around the steering wheel. "Do you think Shannon got a letter?"

Emily licked her lips slowly. Just the sound of her sister's name made her feel sick in the pit of her stomach. She changed the subject quickly, knowing John would be waiting for her. "I'm going to be straight with you – Archie thinks I'm stopping at a hotel with you tonight, but I'm actually staying with John tonight at his house. Do you want to come and meet him? We can have a few drinks and sort both our bloody lives out."

Teresa pulled the keys out of the ignition and smiled at her sister. "Yep, a few bottles of wine will sort anything out. Or at least make us forget our worries for a night. And, yes, I want to meet him, because if you're saying you love this bloke, then I need to make sure he's kosher. I can't believe it – my goody-two-shoes sister head over heels with an ex-con."

Emily smiled. Despite all that had gone down, there was no one like family. Blood *was* thicker.

Chapter Fifteen

John opened the front door and clocked Teresa straight away. His usual confidence seemed to waiver and he gave a half-hearted smile, clearly not sure how she would take him. He ran his fingers through his hair, trying to flatten it down. They all walked into the front room and Teresa was unimpressed as she glanced around. What on Earth was Emily thinking getting mixed up with a dead leg like this? Her sister's home was lovely and, though Teresa hadn't visited for years, Emily had always been so house-proud. Teresa couldn't get her head around her swapping that life for this one.

"I'll make a brew if anyone wants one?" John asked.

Emily sat down and patted the space next to her for Teresa to sit too, but she stayed standing.

She looked at John. "No thanks, I'm going down to the offie to get a few bottles of wine, unless you fancy going for us?"

"Yeah, let me get my clobber together and I'll go. I fancy a pizza or something, too. Are you girls hungry?"

"Yes, I'm starving. Can you get some chips, too, and a garlic bread?" Emily rummaged in her handbag, pulled out some money and held it out to John. "There you go, that should be enough."

Teresa watched John like a hawk as he stepped forward. He took the money and slid it into his back pocket. "Right, I won't be long." He zipped his coat up and shoved his black cap on. "See you soon."

Once the front door banged shut, Emily smiled at her sister. "Come on then, what do you think of him?"

Teresa tried her best to be positive but the look on her face spoke for her. "Bloody hell, Em, I've met him for a few minutes. I don't know anything about the man. When he comes back, I will have a chat with him, see what he's about. But," she paused and looked around the room again. "Is this the life you want? I'm not slagging him off or anything, but he's broke. Look at this place, can you not see what I see?"

"It's not all about money, is it? John excites me. I melt when he looks at me. My heart beats faster. I don't get that with Archie anymore. And on top of all that, after today, I owe him my life. And he's got Gavin off *your* back, too."

"I was sorting that myself, I'll have you know. But I hear you about you and Archie. Everyone thinks the grass is greener on the other side, but maybe if you mowed your own lawn a bit more often you would see what you already have."

"You know what I've been through with Archie, though. You know what he did to me. I don't think I've ever let go of that."

"For crying out loud, woman, that was years ago. If I remember rightly, you were the one who wanted to stay with him back then. I told you to pack his bags and kick his arse out on the street, but no, you were the one who wanted to try and make it work."

"And that's how I felt at the time. Things change. I've changed."

"You've changed because this young stud muffin has given you a bit of attention. I'll tell you what will happen in the future. You'll be skint, he'll be back in the nick, and you will be high and dry wondering how you threw your life away. Money might not buy you happiness, but if you've haven't got any, you're guaranteed to be miserable. And what about work? You'll lose your nice office job, have to graft somewhere else, and I bet he won't get a sniff of a job. You'll go to work every day while he sits at home on his arse doing bugger all?"

Emily folded her arms. "I just want you to be happy for me. You called it earlier – Goody Two Shoes. Well, what if I've had enough – what if I fancy breaking a few rules? You've never played by the book."

Teresa reached for her cigarettes. She sparked one up and sat thinking for a few seconds. "My main concern is you, Emily, and if you're happy then I am. But it's a dangerous game you're playing – and you've got more to lose than me. So do yourself a favour and keep this affair to yourself. Nobody needs to know, at least until you two know this is the real deal."

"It is, it's real. I feel it in my heart."

Teresa shook her head. Emily was such a hopeless romantic and she always looked at things through rose-tinted glasses. She didn't know men like Teresa did, didn't realise they were full of shit when they were getting their ends away. Teresa changed the subject. There had been enough drama for one day – she wanted to keep the peace. "So, are we going to see Mam and Dad then?"

Emily hunched her shoulders. "I've thought about it quite a lot over these last few days and I'm not sure. I wanted to see what you thought. I know what happened was terrible but at the end of the day she's still our mother."

"I know, and that's the hardest part for me. I know what's it like to be a mother who can't see her kid. But," she blew out a breath. "Can I ever sit there in a room with her and forget what she done?"

Emily's voice was softer. "People make mistakes, don't they? Perhaps I never understood it all back then, but I'm in a similar situation now as she might have been. She must have had her reasons for cheating on Dad."

"If it was just the affair, I could forgive her that. I mean, Dad must have. But cheating on him with his best mate – that's low. Do you remember that night he came round and told Dad he'd fight him for Mum? He nearly left Dad for dead. If I close my eyes, I can still see him lying on the floor covered in blood, and she walked past him like he was a dollop of crap on her shoe. And yet he still took her back. I don't get it." Teresa shrugged.

"That's how I feel, too. She did some bad things, let us all down. If she'd sat down with Dad and told him it was over, then at least we all could have come to terms with it together. But she just walked out. Leaving three girls all alone – with Dad passed out and as good as gone. I really thought he was dead. I remember getting blood all over my school uniform trying to wake him up. If he hadn't come round, Social Services would have taken us away."

Teresa stubbed her fag out and sat back in her seat. "Shit happens in life. Fuck knows how many times I've got it wrong. My kid lives with his dad and I sell my body, but I did what I did to give my boy a decent life. She just abandoned us. We basically had to bring each other up – Dad wasn't up to it. So she came waltzing back to him later, but we'd already left home. Not-so-happy families, eh?"

Emily nodded. "I know. And, yet, here I am, doing what she did. Don't get me wrong, I would never, ever, let John lay a finger on Archie, but I'm still unhappy in my marriage. Time's a healer, they say, and maybe we should see her. Let her say her piece. If not for her sake, then for Dad. He forgives her, so maybe we can too."

"You're right, he didn't deserve what happened, and he still gave her a second chance. But, like I said, that's what happens. People make mistakes and sooner or later they realise that. An affair might light a spark, but sparks burn out quick enough."

Emily watched Teresa from the corner of her eye and knew she was having a pop at her.

Luckily, John arrived back. "It's perishing out there. Bleeding freeze the balls off a brass monkey, it would." He placed boxes on the table and took his coat off. "I'll grab some glasses and plates." He carried on the conversation as he got the dishes. "You have another sister, don't you?"

Teresa piped up. "We sure do. Bleeding headache she is too. Always up to no good. After today you might think I'm the problem sister – but wait til you hear about our Shannon. On my life, even from a young age she was a wild one. My mam was always up at school about her behaviour. Tricky bleeder she was, always telling my mam she'd been in school when she clearly hadn't. She's never stopped – she's been playing hooky from us even as an adult. I've not heard a peep from her in years. Texted and called, I did, but no answer."

John smirked. "School is not for everyone, though. Some of us are academic and some of us are – what shall I call it? – hands-on. I'm the hands-on type of guy. I can't stand studying. My head's not made for stuff like that."

Teresa was back at him. "What is it made for, then?"

John shot a look over at Emily and smiled at her. "I'm a go-getter. If I see something I want, I go and get it. I might sometimes have chosen the wrong way to get stuff but, come on, we all do a bit of ducking and diving and wheeling and dealing somewhere along the line, don't we, to earn money? No one's really as innocent as they make out, are they?"

They sat scranning and drinking, the wine taking the edge off the trauma of the day for Emily and Teresa. John stuck to his cans of lager. Teresa licked her fingers and, as the alcohol loosened all their tongues, she wasted no time getting to know John. "What were you in jail for?"

Emily felt her cheeks going red, but John looked unbothered. "Armed robbery. Got caught bang to rights and had the book thrown at me."

"So, are you on the straight and narrow now?" Teresa wasn't wasting a moment.

Emily jumped in quickly to save anything else being said. "John's looking for work. He has had a few days' work here and there but fingers crossed he gets something more permanent soon."

John glared over at Emily. "I have got a mouth, I can speak," he growled.

Teresa noticed the look he gave her sister and carried on with her questions. "So, what's the plan for you and our Em? Are you in love with her? Are you going to treat her right?"

"Crikey, woman – you're worse than the CID. You should have been a bloody detective. We're taking things day by day. We've only just met. Give us a chance, eh?"

Teresa was like a dog with a bone and, even though any other woman would have backed off, she continued. "My sister likes the finer things in life, so you better pull your finger out of your arse and get a job fast."

Emily was chewing on her fingernail nervously and Teresa could see she wanted the floor to open up and swallow her.

"I'll be able to look after her, so wind your neck in and stop going on at me. I've only just met you and already

I think you're judging me. I've not passed comment on how you make a living, have I?"

Now it was Teresa's turn to go red. She started to back-pedal. "John, I'm not judging you. I just love my sister and want to make sure she is going to be fine."

"Yes, and she will be. As far as I know, you two have not seen each other for a long time. It's me who's been making sure Em is alright. Maybe, if you spoke to her, you would realise she's not been happy for a long time. You don't pick who you fall in love with, do you?"

Emily snuggled in closer to John and Teresa watched them both. Maybe she'd overreacted. "John, regardless of anything else, I've not thanked you yet for today. Not many blokes would take on Gav Bloody Turner. He is a nasty bastard and, from what Em says, you gave him a taste of his own medicine. You didn't only save Emily, you got him off my back too. So – I owe you. Gavin Turner has been the bane of my life ever since I took his dirty money."

John nodded. "I've shit bigger than him, love. He won't be giving you any more trouble, that's for sure."

Teresa felt the hairs on the back of her neck stand on end. There was something that unsettled her about the look John had in his eyes. He looked a little too pleased to have had the chance to give someone a beating. She had thought she might stay here tonight but, after talking to John, she knew she would feel safer in a hotel. She casually looked at her watch. "I'm going to get off now, Em. Get a nice little hotel tonight – leave you lovebirds alone. I'll catch up with you tomorrow."

Emily looked surprised. "You can stay here. That's alright, isn't it John?"

"Yep, I'm easy. Do whatever."

But Teresa wanted to be out of here, to be somewhere where no one knew her and she could lock the door on the rest of the world. She stood up and got her belongings together. "I'll have a good sleep, and we can meet up tomorrow and sort out our next move regarding Mam and Dad."

Emily walked her to the front door.

"Bye John, nice meeting you," Teresa shouted back. Emily opened the front door and gave her sister a big hug. "You can stay here, you know, it's not a problem."

"No, honest, I want to have a bath and chill out. My anxiety has been through the roof for these last few days and all I want to do is get in bed and sleep." The hug seemed to last forever before Teresa pulled away. "I'll be back in the morning."

As Emily returned to the front room, John was sitting at the table and he'd put her ten grand on it. She clocked it as soon as she walked back in. John gripped her in a bear hug and kissed the top of her head. "She seemed alright, your kid. A bit outspoken but eh, she's only looking out for you, I guess."

"She's a hothead, our Teresa. She doesn't think before she puts her mouth in gear."

He kissed her fingertips. "We are going to be so happy, you know. Like I said, one last job to get me back on my feet, and me and you will jet off to somewhere nice. Spain maybe? South America? Somewhere hot. What do you think?"

Emily was reluctant to talk about the job he had planned. He glanced at the money on the table and then back at her. "I need to get a few things together for the job, you know, proper kit. With this money I can get clean shooters – proper untraceable."

She swallowed hard and turned her head away.

"Not that I'll need to use them. If I do this right, I wave the gun about and everyone behaves, no one gets hurt. Trust me. I need a grand, money that I will have back to you the moment I get my cut of the job."

She didn't know what to say.

"So… is that a yes then?"

Emily stuttered, "Yes. I mean I have to put the rest of it back in the bank tomorrow. Before Archie checks. But he doesn't know the exact numbers. A grand is fine – if you really think you need to do this job."

John took a bundle of money and rammed it into his back pocket. He winked at Emily and went straight in for a kiss. The force of his lips on hers, his strong hand delving up her t-shirt, were like a drug, blotting out all thought of what they'd discussed. Emily let herself get lost in the moment. She'd face the real world tomorrow. Right now, she was in the arms of the man she loved, her protector, her happy ever after.

Chapter Sixteen

Shannon watched her parents' house from the evening shadows. There was an eerie silence as she looked over the road. The traffic seemed to have disappeared. The other houses all had their curtains closed, no one coming or going. She felt dizzy as she watched the familiar abode. This was her family home. The best of memories and the worst of times all crammed into one location. She focused on the good parts. A warmth ran through her as she managed a smile. The garden looked just the same as it had always done, nothing had changed. Even the hanging baskets were in the same place. The memories of hot summers lying in the garden with her sisters, water fights, cartwheel practices, all came flooding back. The garden was always a happy place for Shannon. The family would often light a barbecue there and have a few beers on hot summer nights, chatting to the neighbours, music spilling out from other houses. Shannon looked up to the window at the top left of the house. She wrapped her arms around herself as she remembered standing on tiptoes, looking out of that exact window as a child. For hours she would stand there watching the world go by, singing, thinking, chasing raindrops down the glass. But that bedroom held bad memories too. And one in particular that she'd shut away for years. If you told yourself hard enough that something didn't happen, you could nearly believe it. Until you were standing there, facing that place again.

She'd given birth in that room. After a full nine months of keeping it a secret – first from her family and then from the outside world – she'd shamed them all, shamed herself. She'd spent her pregnancy feeling guilty, terrified, trapped. But when she finally had the baby, there in the front bedroom, for a moment it had all felt worth it. She wanted to keep the baby, hold her in her arms, take no notice of the comments about her being young, being unmarried. But, no, her father insisted there would be no more shame brought on his family, his name. After their mum left, he'd had an edge to him. She'd begged him, pleaded with him on bended knee to let her keep her baby, but he wouldn't listen to a word she said. It was Teresa who helped him make the decision. She told Shannon she was a slut and having the baby taken from her was her penance for having sex with a married man. No one listened to Shannon. They took her baby away and left her crying in her room for months after it was gone.

She would have been a good mother. She would have changed her ways, found a job, got her own house. To this day, an emptiness gripped her heart, a feeling that never left her. Everyone expected her to get on with things after her child was taken, get things back to bloody normal, her father said, but nobody ever asked her how she was doing, how her mental health was. And she would have told them how she felt, told them she wanted her baby, told them they could all fuck off, but back then she was barely an adult in name only. She might have had a baby but she felt as small and terrified as a lost child.

Shannon walked slowly over the road, not sure if she wanted to continue. A cold shiver ran down her spine as she touched the cold iron gate. Her knuckles turned white as she pushed it open, the edge of it scraping on the floor. It was like her feet were glued to the floor, no strength in her legs, all the hurt and pain from days gone by rushing into her body. No, she could never face her parents again. She quickly turned around and was about to walk away. What the hell was she even thinking coming here?

Then a voice from behind her, a familiar tone. "Shannon, is that you?"

Her mouth went dry. She slowly turned back around. She stayed still as a statue as he rushed towards her, his arms enveloping her in a bear-hug. "I knew you would come first. I said to your mam, our Shannon will come, I did, on my life, I said those exact words." He released his grip and pulled back to look at her. His expression changed as though asking himself, where were her chubby, rosy cheeks, her big blue eyes, her thick hair? His warm hand gripped hers. "Come on, you look perished. Let's go inside and warm you up."

Shannon never said a word. She went along with what he said, just like she'd always done. The heat hit her as she walked in through the front door. It was always a warm house and, when she was growing up, she'd liked to throw open the doors to let the air in. Her dad led her straight into the kitchen and pulled a chair out. He flicked the kettle on and took two cups out of the cupboard. "A nice cup of tea will warm you up. Is it still two sugars?"

Shannon nodded, amazed he remembered how she liked her cuppa. She looked around the room, digesting everything. She examined the pine table and smiled as she clocked the deep line in it. She did that. Yep, she'd dug her key deep into the wood once when she was upset. She slowly stroked the small dint and closed her eyes. If this table could have spoken, it would have told her family how sad she'd been, how her heart had broken and how many tears she'd cried sitting at it in the late hours when they were all tucked up in bed.

Sam stirred the cuppas and sat down next to her. "You've not said a word, love, are you alright?"

Her dad was like that – he'd always smooth over the truth. He'd ask questions but never want to hear the answers. He'd find a way of brushing something under the carpet rather than talk about it properly.

Shannon cupped her hands around the white mug and sipped a small mouthful. This was her chance to say everything that was in her heart, to stand up and yell that she wasn't alright, that she'd never been alright ever since they took her baby away. But the words wouldn't come. "I'm fine, Dad, just a bit strange being sat here with you, that's all. Have the others been in touch?"

"Nope, not a bloody call, a text, a letter, nothing."

Shannon felt ashamed that a wave of relief flooded her. Facing her parents was one thing: facing her sisters was a whole different ball game. She took her coat off and hung it on the back of her chair.

Her father's eyes widened and his jaw dropped. "Bleeding hell, you're all skin and bones."

She pulled at her jumper and tried to hide her skinny body. He clocked the bruises on her wrist. He reached over and rolled the cuff of her sleeve up so he could get a better look. "Bruises, where are they from?"

Shannon's eyes filled with tears, years of emotions bubbling at the back of her throat. "Don't, Dad," she said quietly as she rolled her sleeve back down.

"What do you mean 'don't'? You're covered in bruises, and you expect me to be quiet? Not a bloody chance. Where are they from?"

Shannon reached into her coat pocket and pulled out her fags. She lit one with a shaking hand. If she was going to talk about her life, then she'd rather start now and work backwards. For all the pain Paddy had caused her, it was easier to say his name than mention the baby.

Sam was waiting on her answer, eyes never leaving her face.

"It was some guy I was with, and, before you start, I've left him and I know I've been a dickhead without you telling me. God knows, I know."

Sam shook his head. It had always been the same with Shannon: she was always attracted to the bad boys. Even from an early age, she was in the mix with the older lads on the estate. He'd threatened to chin anyone who gossiped about his youngest daughter. He denied Shannon was the girl all the neighbourhood was talking about and told anyone who blackened her name he would put them ten feet under. But when she told him she was pregnant, he knew it had all been true. He stared at Shannon now. The dark circles under her eyes, deep wrinkles around her mouth, she'd aged in a way that showed suffering. "Shan, how many times have we talked about your self-worth? You need to know your worth and realise how you should be treated by any man. Don't be anybody's doormat."

"Dad, I didn't set out to end up in a relationship like that. It happens over time. And as time went on it got worse and worse. Lesson learned, eh?"

"I bloody hope so, love. I've always worried about you the most, you know."

"You don't need to worry about me. I'm a big girl now and, as long as I have a single breath left in my body, I'll never, ever, let anybody treat me like I've been treated again. I've seen the light. Once bitten, twice shy." She stared at her father and tried to say the even bigger things, but the words stayed stuck in her chest.

Neither of them spoke for a few seconds. Sometimes silence was golden. Shannon decided facing up to the truth about her mother's illness was easier than facing the truth of her past. "How's my mam?"

Sam bit down on his bottom lip, hard. "Not good, love. She has good days and bad days, but lately the bad days are outweighing the good."

"Is it lung cancer?"

"Yeah, incurable. The doc said it could be three to six months before," he paused, and his bottom lip started to tremble. "Before she leaves us."

"Come on, Dad, don't be getting upset. My mam has always been a fighter and I can't see her giving up til the bitter end."

"It's been hard, love, very hard. She's fading away in front of my eyes. I don't know how I stand up straight anymore. She's my world, my life, always has been."

Shannon wanted to remind him of the past and how her mother had left him for his best friend, the same man who had beaten him senseless, but it wasn't the time. She would never kick a man while he was down.

"We can go up and see her when you've finished your drink, if you want. She'll be over the moon that you have come."

Shannon nodded and picked up her tea. "Let me drink this first. I don't know if I'm ready to see her, Dad. After all these years. My nerves are shattered at the moment. I am staying at a women's refuge, and they are helping me sort my life out. My head has been in bits with it all. Paddy, my ex, will not rest until he finds me, and I know sooner or later I will have to face him."

Sam rounded his fists into two tight balls and slammed one on the table. "I'll deal with him if he comes anywhere near you. I might be an old man, but I've still got a punch on me."

"Violence isn't the answer, Dad. I had to learn the hard way, like I had to all my life. You can't fight heartbreak with your fists, and you can't outrun your pain." She locked eyes with Sam and they both knew what she was talking about. But even now, she could never ask if he was sorry for making her give her baby up, if he knew it broke her heart into a thousand pieces that she'd never be able to fix.

The tension was broken by the sound of a rasping cough from upstairs. Sam hurried out of the room and headed up the stairs with his daughter close behind him.

Brenda was motionless as Sam opened the bedroom door. He crept inside and sat on the edge of the bed. He whispered, "Bren, open your eyes, love. Shannon's come to see you."

Shannon stood at the bedroom door, unsure of what to do.

Sam beckoned her inside. "Come on, love. Come and sit here. I'll move up." He patted the bed.

She took a deep breath and sat on the bed. She looked at her mother for the first time in years. "Mam." Shannon laid her head on her mother's chest and her shoulders started shaking as she sobbed her heart out. A hand rested on top of her head and slowly stroked her hair.

Brenda tried her best to sit up. Shannon stood up and helped her, propping pillows behind her head. That was better, they could look at each other now. A mother's touch was a powerful thing and Shannon's presence had brought energy back to the frail woman. Brenda examined every inch of her daughter's face, stroking her fingers over her cheeks, her lips, her forehead. It was like she was memorising every contour on Shannon's face.

"You've changed, baby girl, got thinner," Brenda said in a low voice.

"I've missed your cooking, that's why, Mam. I need some of your chocolate cakes down my neck to put a bit of timber on me."

Brenda squeezed her daughter's hand again. "I don't think I will make another cake, love. It's down to you now to be the one who bakes. Something sweet even when life is bitter." Brenda knew her daughter had suffered bad times, just by looking at her. No more words needed saying. Brenda pulled her closer until Shannon was more or less lying on the bed next to her mother.

This was all too much for Sam and he quietly left the room.

"I've missed you, Shannon, missed you and your sisters every single day you've not been here. I know what I did was wrong and if I could turn back time I would. I got caught up in something and couldn't get back out of it. Your dad is a wonderful man, and I should never have betrayed his trust like that."

"It was horrible, Mam. We thought he was dead the night you left him and, even when the cuts and bruises healed, he couldn't function without you. He certainly couldn't bring up three headstrong girls on his own. We were all broken that day you went."

"I know, baby girl, I know. I can't change what has happened, I can only tell you from the bottom of my heart how much I love your dad and my girls. I have hated myself for what I did. Every day I've tortured myself with the guilt I have in my heart."

Shannon didn't have anything to say in reply. She had rehearsed exactly what she would say to her mother if their paths ever crossed, but sat here, looking at her, all the anger seemed to have subsided, and her words had dried up. "Mam, you don't have to explain anymore. We've all got regrets. It's now that matters, and getting you comfortable now is all I care about."

Brenda turned her eyes away from her daughter and looked out of the window at the night sky. It was easier to stare into the dark than talk about the past.

Shannon dried her tears and looked directly into her mother's eyes when she finally turned back. "It's been so hard without you, Mam. I've been to hell and back and had nobody to turn to. I missed out on my own chance to be a mother. I tried to fill the void inside me with booze and pills. I chased the worst men – the ones I thought were strong but really were nothing but bullies and vindictive bastards. Do you think it's God paying me back for what I done? I often think he is because why else would I have to live my life like I have been doing?"

"Stop being silly, love. This is a new chapter for you and, although I can't change what has happened to you in the past, perhaps I can change what happens to you in the future. When your sisters arrive, and I pray they will, I will tell you all together about my plans. But please promise me you will never go back to this man who's been hurting you. You're free of it."

Shannon stared at the wall in front of her and nodded. "I'm going to make a fresh start. Me and Frank."

"Frank?" Brenda looked puzzled.

"My dog. He's been the only thing keeping me going. He's in a foster home until I get sorted out. I need to find a place to stay where he can come too."

"You can come back here, love. Move back here with us. Your dad would be glad of the company. And," she paused. "The time will come when I won't be here and he'll need you by his side. He will need you all."

Shannon felt another wave of tears coming. "Mam, you can't leave us. I need you; we all need you. We've got so much to say, so many ghosts to lay to rest."

"I wish I could stay, love. I wish more than anything I had time on my side, but the truth is I won't be here much longer. It's only waiting to see you and your sisters, so I can clear my conscience, that's given me a reason to hang on this long. The doctors have tried all they can. I'm in God's hands now."

Chapter Seventeen

Emily sat in a world of her own staring at the television in the lounge. She should have been upstairs doing her make-up, curling her hair. Teresa would be here soon. They were planning a night out in town, late-night shopping, a few drinks. Jena was coming along too – it was meant to be a celebration of getting back in touch, yet her mind was a million miles away.

Archie came into the room and plonked down near her. "So, off you all go. I'll sit here on my Jacks and do fuck all as per. Yeah, you go out with the girls again. Don't give me a second thought."

Emily turned to him and shook her head, not in the mood for his complaining. "Read a book, clean out that junk cupboard in the hallway like you've been saying you will do for the last year. Or better still, get some paint out and give this place a freshen up. All you do lately is follow me around and badger my head. Get a life, will you? Do your own thing and get off my bleeding back."

Archie looked sour, fed up with his wife and her new attitude. She'd always been the one to stay at home, keeping the place tidy while he went out with the lads of an evening. He wasn't liking it now the boot was on the other foot.

Jena came in, ready to go. She looked nice in her faded flared jeans and a white belly top. "Mam, are you not ready yet? I thought you said Teresa would be here soon?"

Emily stood up and stretched her arms over her head. "I am ready, you cheeky mare. I just need to shove some make-up on."

Jena looked her mother up and down. "Mam, go and put something different on. We're going for drinks in the bars on Deansgate, not nipping to the bloody corner shop. Everyone dresses up, so go and put a bit of slap on, and tidy your hair up. I thought you had turned a corner with the way you were dressing."

Archie tried again. "I've just said I've not been invited, Jen, what do think about that?"

"It's not happening, Dad. This is a girls' night. Why don't you watch a bit of footy or something?" Jena chuckled.

There was knocking at the front door. Jena went to answer it.

"Oh, you look lovely," Teresa said to her.

"And so do you. My mam's getting changed and then we should be ready to go. Just a heads-up, my dad is after coming along with us. Please tell him no," she giggled.

Teresa walked into the house and Jena followed closely behind her. "That perfume is lovely, what is it?" She went right up to her auntie and sniffed her neck. "It smells like holidays."

Teresa smiled. "It's called Black Vanilla by Mancera. I love their stuff. There's nothing else like it if you want to stand out. I've always loved new fragrances. Ever since I was a young girl, perfume has always been my thing."

Emily walked back into the room. "Yep, perfume, bags, make-up, clothes, shoes, coats. She always had the largest collection of everything when we were growing up. And God help anyone who ever touched any of her belongings without asking her. She would have scratched your eyes out."

Teresa smiled at her sister, remembering how protective she had been about her belongings. "You look nice, sis."

Jena burst out laughing. "Yeah, she does now. I've just sent her back upstairs to get changed. I told her straight: we are out to impress today. I could be meeting my Prince Charming. You never know, do you?"

Keys jingling, Emily hooked her handbag over her shoulder and took one last look in the mirror. "I'm ready to go. Come on, ladies let's hit those bars. Archie, I'll be back when I'm back, don't wait up."

Jena gave him a big hug. "You have a rest day, Dad. We'll be back before you know it."

Archie squeezed his daughter and said, "No kiss from my wife, then?"

Emily shot a look at Teresa and rolled her eyes. "Bleeding hell, Archie, I'm going out for a few drinks not leaving the bloody country."

A few drinks in, Emily could feel the buzz kicking in. Jena was on her phone on the other side of the bar. All night long her mobile had been ringing and Emily had already pointed out that she was never off it. It was rude, in her eyes. But Teresa clocked they had a moment to speak openly and moved in closer to her sister. "Have you spoken to John today?"

"He keeps messaging me, but I've not replied yet. I was going to go and meet him tonight, but how can I when Jena decided to come with us? Teresa, my head is all over at the moment. He keeps asking me to move in with him. I can't simply up and leave Archie, can I?"

"You know how I feel, but you've got to make your own mind up. If you are going all-in, you'd better do the groundwork first. Maybe you should mention something to Jena about things not being too good at home. Because," she paused. "If the shit hits the fan, she needs to be prepared, doesn't she? Look at us when Mam and Dad split up. We were all devoed. I thought they were the happiest couple I knew. Never in a million years would I have guessed my mam was playing away from home."

Emily nodded in agreement. "But I can understand Mam a bit now I'm older. She wanted passion in her marriage, for Dad to tell her he still fancied her, wanted to rip her clothes off her back."

Teresa burst out laughing. "Thats's not an image I ever want of Mum and Dad."

Emily was laughing too now. "No seriously, you know what I mean. Just because you marry someone, it doesn't mean you don't have urges, needs."

"So, you spice it up then. You say he's boring, but you must play a part in it too. Do you ever have sex anywhere other than the bedroom? Maybe outside, or in the car?"

Emily shook her head. "Do I eckers. It's never been like that with us. It's always in the bedroom, nowhere else."

"So change it up. Listen, you know the job I do. Working with men and what they want in the bedroom is my forté. If I had a pound for every man who is bored at home, I would be a very rich woman indeed. You talk about your urges, but men are dirty bastards, end of. Sure, they like sexy underwear and all the raunchy stuff but, if I'm being really honest, they also like a lot of stuff they won't ask their wives for. I'm talking putting your tongue where the sun don't shine. I can give you loads of tips to fix your marriage, if that's what you want? Come on, what does John give you that Archie doesn't? Because clearly it's not money and gifts. If it's sex, well, like I said, that can be sorted. But if it's danger, you're on your own with that."

Emily leaped to his defence. "He said, when he gets back on his feet, he will take me away for romantic weekends and all that."

Teresa looked sceptical. "Believing it is one thing, seeing it is another. I get that you think you love him, but be careful. Don't you be the one funding all these dates and buying him clothes and all that, because I bet you have already, haven't you?"

"I have bought him a few shirts, that's all. Stuff he needed for job interviews."

"Job interviews? He doesn't look the suit-and-tie type to me, Em. What about cash, have you given him any money?"

Emily felt glad of the low lighting in the bar. It was easier to lie without the cold light of day on her. "Nope, I haven't given him any money. What do you take me for? Listen, Teresa, I'm not doing it for the money, or the security. I'm doing this for me."

Teresa knew that determined tone in Emily's voice. "Right, you get going and I'll stay here with Jena. I'll tell her some of your mates from work were in here and they asked you to go on somewhere with them. You go and see Loverboy."

Emily was already finishing her drink and hooking her handbag over her shoulder. She kissed her sister once on her cheek and looked her straight in the eyes. "Thanks, sis, love you." And she was gone.

Teresa watched Jena on the other side of the room. She looked as shifty as hell. She was finally off the phone, but now she was in a corner with some girls. It all happened so fast and, if Teresa hadn't known what to look for, she'd have thought it was just another group of girls on a night out. But she watched her niece shake hands with one the girls. What teenage girl shook hands? Blink and you would have missed it. She watched Jena going in for hugs, dipping into her handbag then throwing her arms around these other girls. Now you see it, now you don't.

Teresa stood up and wove her away across the bar towards her niece. Jena was on the phone again. She had started dancing where she was stood. Teresa joined her.

"You've been gone ages. Your mam has gone too. A couple of her workmates were begging her to go with them to a party and I told her to go. Come on, let's go to a club, and I'll show you how I roll."

Jena was looking around her all the time, on edge. "Yeah, erm, sure. Let's stay here for a bit first though. I like the vibe in here, great music."

Teresa nodded and found a table nearby. The music was alright but not what she would have chosen; baseline pumping, and she couldn't make out a word the singer said. Maybe she was getting old. But not so old she couldn't see what Jena was doing. Teresa watched her niece, now stood with a couple of guys. Jena passed the man two small packages and then he handed over some money. It didn't take much to put two and two together. This girl never really worked yet, to hear her mother talk, she was always buying new clothes and stuff. It all made sense now. She was licking shot.

Jena turned and her eyes opened wide as she clocked her auntie staring daggers at her. "I'm ready now, shall we go to the club?"

Teresa gripped Jena by the arm and dragged her away from the group. "So, that's what you are, a fucking drug dealer? At first, I just thought you were very popular in here, then the penny dropped. Bleeding hell, you must think I've got 'prat' written all over my head."

Jena was in a panic. "Teresa, I only sell a bit of sniff to get some extra money. At first, I earned enough to buy the odd dress for a night out and that, but when I realised how much I could earn doing this full-time, it was a no-brainer.

There is no way I'm going to work in some poxy office all week for shit money when I can do what I'm doing and have a cushdy life."

Teresa shuddered. It was like hearing herself speak back when she was a teenager looking for fast money. "You will get hurt, love. This is a dangerous world to be in. People are probably watching you as we speak, and it will only be a matter of time before they try and have you over. That's how it works, that's how it's always worked. There's a reason why they get kids like you doing this, selling gear for the big boys – it's because you'll either get nicked, addicted or done over by the competition before too long, and they'll find the next young girl to take your place. Sort your head out and get a bleeding job. Your mam will go sick if she gets wind of this. And, trust me, if you carry on, I will be telling her."

Jena's look changed and she stepped closer to Teresa, nose-to-nose. "No one will tell her. We have all done things to get what we need, so back off." Teresa was taken aback; she'd never seen this side to her niece. "So, go on then, what do you want me to do? Stop selling drugs and be skint? Sit around at home listening to my mam and dad fighting? Nah, I'll do this for a bit until I've got enough to move out. Then it won't be anyone's business but my own how I earn a dollar."

"I want you to be safe, Jena, for crying out loud. Listen to me, will you? I've lived in this world a few more decades than you, and I know from first-hand experience that it's very dangerous. Who do you deal for? Go on, I bet it's some local gangster you're screwing."

Jena clearly didn't want to have this conversation anymore. "I've known the guy a long time, for your information, and he treats me well."

"So, you sniff too? Come on, you don't sell sniff and not dabble in it yourself. Bleeding hell, this is getting worse by the minute."

Jena grabbed her auntie by the hand and led her outside. It was bitterly cold, glittering patterns of frost already creeping over the pavements. Jena leaned against a brick wall and reached inside her handbag for her cigarettes. She passed one to Teresa and flicked the lighter underneath it.

"Go on then, let's hear it, because I'll tell you straight, at the moment all I want to do is knock your bleeding block off and take you home to your mother."

Jena sucked a hard drag from her fag and blew it out before she replied. "I only used to have a few bumps at the weekend and, honestly, I never ever paid for it. Mike always gave it me for nothing, said it would help me have a better night. And, in all fairness, it did. I was confident, bouncing around the joint with loads of energy, the life and soul of the party."

There was no need to tell Teresa what life was like when you were sniffing cocaine, because she already knew all about it. Of course, she had done her fair share in the past. She was an escort who attended all the best parties, weekends away with rich men and all of them used the white powder. But it had always been a work thing for her – something to keep her the life and soul of the party. The moment she had felt it get out of control she had gone cold turkey. "So, are you addicted then? I don't mean like some mugshot of a junkie – I mean do you feel like you need it, like you have to take it every day?"

A single tear trickled down Jena's cheek and landed on her lip. She lifted her head. "I think so. It used to just be nights out, but now I have it every day to give me some energy. Mike said I'm not hooked, but I think I am. I can't focus without it, feel like shit when I'm not high."

Teresa choked up listening to her niece's story. "I will help you get off that shit. I'll tell this Mike guy to fuck off, you're not selling it any more. Let him get off his arse and do his own dirty work."

Jena was looking down at her toes. "I wish it was as easy as that. I owe him money; he said I have to work it off. I know already what you are going to say, so don't waste your breath telling me I've been an idiot."

This story was familiar to Teresa, way too familiar. What the hell had happened to her family? She should have been around, then her niece would have never got herself in this mess to start with. "I'm gutted Jena, honest. I should have protected you from all of this. I should have been here to support your mam, but I was so wrapped up in my own little world and my own shit that I neglected you all. Fuck me, can this get any worse?"

Jena swallowed hard and nodded slowly. "You're going to go ape when I tell you, but hear me out. I have been sleeping with men for money. I don't know how I got involved – it just happened. Mike had a friend who he said was going through a hard time and he offered me money to go on a date with him, you know, to cheer him up and all that. Teresa placed her hand on her shoulder and encouraged her to continue. "Mike gave me a couple of hundred quid for it. Easy money, I thought, especially when I was skint. The guy was a bit older than me, but, in all fairness, he was alright-looking. We had a great night and one thing led to another and we slept together."

"That's not too bad. Loads of girls go out at the weekend and have a one-night stand. I have lots of mates who do that."

"I know, and that's what I told myself after it happened. Anyway, Mike started saying the same thing to me all the time, you know? He had a mate who was down in the dumps, having relationship troubles and all that, and he offered me the same deal with each date I went on. I never really cottoned on what was happening. I focused on the money I was earning and, before I knew it, I was seeing three or four guys a week."

"It's a world that's hard to walk away from, love. I'm going to tell you something now, something only a few people know about me. I've been an escort since I was your age. Your mam has only just found out. I'm not going to judge you, because I've been in the same boat. All I can do is help you. I mean, I take it you do want to stop, don't you?"

Jena's bottom lip trembled and her voice was low. "I don't know, I can't think straight anymore. If I don't work, I can't pay my debt back."

Jena was sobbing and Teresa put a loving arm around her. "Come on, come back to my hotel room and we can sort this mess out. I promise you, everything will be fine. There'll be no more drugs in your life, and this Mike guy can piss right off. I've dealt with his sort all my life. Trust me, he won't bother you no more after I've spoken to him."

Chapter Eighteen

John jumped as Emily walked into the room. He was fuming. "Fucking hell, you said you would be here hours ago. I hate waiting about, it does my head in."

Emily placed the white envelope on the table and sat down next to John. "I'm sorry. Jena decided to join us and I couldn't get away. But I'm here now. That's what matters, isn't it? And I've brought the cash you asked for. Though I don't get it – I thought the grand I gave you the other day was all you needed to set the job up?"

"Quit worrying – I'll have it back to you as soon as this job pulls off."

"John, you know I've never judged you for your past. But are you sure you want to be getting involved in this world again? We've had this conversation time and time again, but I can't help worrying about you."

John spoke through gritted teeth. "Fuck me, woman, are you not listening when I tell you about all the things I want to do when I've got a few quid in my back pocket?

Honest, I thought you had your head screwed on and were onboard with all this. If you're only playing bad boys with me, I'm done."

"I have got my head screwed on; I care about you, that's all. What are you going to do? Shoot me for caring, why don't you."

"If you cared that much about me, you would have told your husband by now, wouldn't you?"

Emily was stuck for words. John was being so nasty, and over these last few days she'd noticed a change in the way he'd been speaking to her. Every other message was either a request for cash or some snide comment about whether she'd told Archie yet. "John, let's not argue. We've got all evening together – Teresa's covering for me. Come here. I've been thinking about what you do to me…"

"I'm not in the mood. It's all doing my head in, this situation. I need to do this job, then I can think straight again. I've been texting a few of my boys and I think they've got the stuff I need. Now I've got the cash, I can get over there and do the deal."

Emily felt a wave of disappointment and fear. "Be careful, John. I don't want to know the details of what you are doing or what you're buying from who, I only want you home safe. Text me or ring me when you're back and I'll come over."

"See what I mean? You should be here waiting for me. We are a team, or so I thought. I want you here with me tonight, in my bed, when I get back, like my woman should be."

Emily reached for him, but he pulled away. "John, I want to be with you as much as you want to be with me. Be patient."

John growled, "Fucking patient, are you having a laugh? Don't ever tell me to be patient, darling. I've been patient for years – waiting for the day I was freed. You're forgetting I can walk away and get any bird I want on my arm, and she'd come with no baggage."

He was deliberately rattling her cage now. "No need to be speaking to me like this, John. We both knew when we started out seeing each other what we were getting into. And, as for you getting another bird on your arm, if that's what you want, crack on. Pay me the money back you owe me, and I'll be gone."

Silence. Emily wondered if she'd pushed him too far.

"Sorry babes," he whispered. His warm lips moved into hers and he passionately kissed her. "I always get like this when I'm planning a job. But stick with me and I should be wadded soon enough. Then I can start to show you what a good time really is. Make sure your passport is in date. Our new life will be waiting for us."

As the potential reality of it all hit home, Emily felt goose-bumps rising on her arms. Was she really ready for this? Did John really mean what he said? This had been fun while it was all just talk but, if he was off to buy a shooter tonight, she had better face facts.

"I can't wait here for you. Not tonight. Text me when you're back – I need to know you're home, not dead in a gutter somewhere."

John didn't seem bothered that she was leaving. He was counting out the money from the envelope and putting it in neat piles across the table. "Yeah, ring me later."

Emily sat in the bus-stop over the road from John's house, wishing she'd driven instead. It was freezing and the next bus was fifteen minutes' wait. She was thinking about calling a cab when a blonde lady walked past her in a hurry. Emily watched her cross the road and stop at John's house. John appeared at the door, silhouetted against the light. Emily couldn't make out what they were saying, and she had half a mind to go running over there, but something held her back. John spoke to the woman for at least five minutes before he hugged her goodbye and shut the door.

Emily watched the woman walk off in the other direction, and was alone again. More lost than ever.

Chapter Nineteen

The next day, Shannon sat with her mother all day. It was good to talk about the good times. She'd come here with scores to settle but, right now, they all needed the comfort of happier memories. She had forgotten how much love was held in her family home and she felt safe being here compared to life with Paddy. She'd not felt safe for a very long time. Paddy had always drummed it into her that he would protect her, but his version of protection was locking her away from the world. She had planned for such a long time what she was going to do when she was free, but now the day was here, the future felt too big to think about. It was easier to be here, wrapped up in her past.

Brenda checked the old brass carriage clock at the side of her bed and knew it was time for Shannon to be heading back to the refuge before curfew. She held her daughter's hand tightly and looked into her eyes. "I don't think the girls are going to come to see me, are they?"

Shannon couldn't meet her gaze. "Mam, all you need to do is think about getting better. The girls know you want to see them, so the ball is their court, isn't it?"

Brenda cringed and shook her head. "I'm not going to get better, love. I've told you – you don't need to protect me. The doctors have already said, this is the end for me."

"Ssh Mam, stop talking like that. I know lots of people who the docs have written off and they have gone on to live for years. Doctors talk through their arses sometimes."

"I hope I'm one of them people they got it wrong about, love, but look at me, Shannon, this isn't living, I'm just existing. I have been ill for a long time, and I owe it to your dad not to hang on to life any longer than I have to. I want to set him free. He's been caring for me for what seems like eternity. He's had no life. Day in day out he's been looking after me. He bathes me, combs my hair and feeds me. I hate him having to do that."

"That's what you do when you love somebody, Mam. For better for worse, until death us do part and all that."

"I know, but I've already tested his oaths to the limit – haven't I? He took me back and how have I repaid him? I see the sadness in his eyes every day. He has no life; he doesn't go down to the pub with his pals anymore, and I've told him time and time again I will be fine. He won't even go to the shops without getting a neighbour to sit with me." Brenda swallowed hard and wriggled to sit upright. "I've always loved him, Shannon, I never meant to hurt him – I just had my head turned. And then it got nasty, and I couldn't come back – not until, well, until it was too late to be there for you girls. And for the record, I know it was you I hurt the most. If I'd been at home, I could have helped you keep the baby. But your dad would never have allowed it given the circumstances," her eyes widened as she continued.

Shannon hated even thinking about it. "It's me who's paid for it every day in heartache. Why is it always the women who suffer? He was just as much to blame as I was, Mam. I was drunk and in no fit state to make any kind of decision. It was just one night, just the one time. Yes, we'd flirted for ages – I liked the attention, I admit. But he was the one who came on to me. I didn't even remember it properly, if I'm being honest, and yet I'm the one who got all the shit for it. I've had to keep my mouth closed for years and for what? To protect him? I tried to block it out, tried to stop thinking about my baby, but how could I when—"

The bedroom door opened. Sam stood there, and Shannon wasn't sure if he had heard what they were talking about. He walked over to the bed and kissed Brenda on the top of her head. "It's time for your rest, love. Me and Shannon can go and have a cuppa while you have a nap." Sam was right, Brenda was tired and her medication was kicking in. Shannon dried the tears from the corner of her eyes.

Shannon was already putting her coat on when Sam came into the front room. "I thought you were going to have a brew, love. You're not going, are you?"

"Yeah, Dad. I want to get the early bus before it goes dark. If I miss it, I'll have to wait another forty minutes before the next one comes."

"I'll run you back if you want?"

"No, I'll be fine. The refuge don't like you telling anybody where you live. It's like a safeguarding rule they have in place to protect us women."

"Before you go, can I have a quick word with you?"

Shannon fidgeted, no eye contact. "What about? I have to go, Dad. I've just told you I will miss the bus."

"I heard what you were saying to your mam, and I know you hated me for what I made you do back then, but it was for the best. For everyone."

Shannon was already walking to the door. This was a conversation she never wanted to have with her old man. No, she could never open that can of worms with him. "Maybe another time, Dad, my head's not with it today. Come here and give me a kiss before I go." They hugged and Shannon planted her lips on her father's cheek. She pulled back and looked him in the eyes. "I hope Teresa and Emily come before it's too late. She doesn't look well, does she? Her breathing is getting worse."

"I know." Sam sat on the arm of the sofa and dropped his head into his hands, his shoulders shaking. "I know it will be soon. I keep lying to myself, telling myself she's getting better but, each day that goes by, I am losing another piece of her. I can't stand watching her in pain any longer. It's tearing me apart inside. I wish your sisters would come. Then I would know, if she goes, she would be at peace."

"It's a big ask, Dad. Nobody can make them come – not after everything we went through."

"I know, love, but my biggest fear is they come too late. I'm going to go to Emily's tomorrow, just turn up. If she turns me away, then so be it. I have to try. I'll do anything to get all my girls back together."

Shannon sucked hard on her bottom lip – she knew her dad was waiting for her to offer to intervene. Like that would help. "Got to go, Dad, I'll be back tomorrow."

"I love you," he said as he watched her leave.

Shannon stood at the empty bus-stop. She had told her dad she would miss the bus and it looked like she had been right. She pulled her jacket up over her nose to lessen the reek of the place, then stuck her head out from the shelter and checked down the long road for any sign of the bus. Nothing. She sparked up a cigarette and stared out into the darkness.

A silhouette approached from the other side of the road, swaying one way then the other. She stood back and took another drag from her fag in a world of her own, thinking about the past.

"Hello, baby. Told you I would find you."

Shannon's throat constricted as the man pulled down the scarf wrapped around his mouth. Her heartbeat doubled, every hair on her body standing on end.

"Move away from me, Paddy. I swear you come near me, and I'll ring the fucking dibble. They've told you you're not allowed near me, so why would you risk getting arrested? Idiot, you are, brain dead."

"Because I never break a promise. I told you I would search the ends of the Earth for you and it didn't take a fucking rocket scientist to work out where you would end up. Aw, did little baby girl go and see Mammy and Daddy? Did they cuddle you and tell you everything would be alright?"

Shannon backed into the corner of the shelter as he approached her. He was drunk, eyes dancing with madness. Shannon knew she was in danger and there was not a soul around. She could have screamed but nobody would have heard her.

"Paddy, I loved you with all my heart and it was you who ruined it. You who spoiled the love we had."

"Go on, tell me you don't love me anymore. Say it, go on."

Shannon could tell by his eyes he was waiting for her to say something he could blame her for, before pummelling his fists into her. She'd played this game with him more than once. "I love the old Paddy, the one I fell for, not the person you are today. You've turned into a monster, someone I don't recognise anymore."

His voice changed: "A monster, am I? Well, I'll prove you wrong. Come back home with me and I'll forgive you. I'll put all this behind us and we can start again."

Shannon shook her head, hands dug deep in her coat pocket. "No Paddy, I'm not coming home. My mother is ill, and I want to be with her."

She stepped forward, but he put his hand in front of her, blocking her path. "Don't you move, Shan. Nah, don't think you can bin me off just like that. I've put time and effort into finding you and you're coming home with me, whether you like it or not."

He was in her face now, eyes bulging from their sockets. She had to think quick before she didn't have a choice anymore. But it was too late, he gripped her hair and swung her face into the metal bars of the bus shelter. She dropped to the floor like a sack of spuds, blood squirting from her nose. He kept her pushed back in the corner so nobody could see her. Paddy was wild, kicking her now, just like the old days, just like he did when he couldn't get his own way. "Paddy, get away from me, leave me alone," she pleaded. He was like a man possessed.

She'd wrapped her arms over her head to shield her face, but through her fingers she saw a pair of feet approaching. Before they got too close, she saw the person veer away. Someone who didn't want any part of this, who'd decided this was none of his business. Shannon thought about yelling out, but it would have only made things worse. Paddy hadn't seen him, and it was a good job because he would have dealt with him too.

Shannon lay curled up on the cold floor, body shaking. Paddy was finally spent, his rage burned out. He slumped down and sat by her, stroking her head. "You should have listened to me. I told you to come home with me, then everything would have been fine. But you didn't listen, you didn't fucking listen."

Chapter Twenty

"I've told you I can't give you any more money, John. It's not my fault the deal didn't come off. I've already given you all the cash I can spare and, if Archie finds out money is missing from the bank, he will be asking questions."

He sneered, "Like I'm arsed about what that prick thinks. Tell him to come and see me if he wants to know where the money is. I'll fucking one-bomb him."

Emily perched on the arm of the sofa next to John. "And you've missed your appointment at probation today. I'll have to send you a warning."

He screwed his face up and let out a sarcastic laugh. "Send me what you want, love. Like a piece of paper is going to bother me."

Emily felt panic fluttering like a bird in her chest. To say this relationship had gone off course was an understatement. John was angry all the time and, since he'd started smoking weed again, she knew where her money was going. The weed was something he'd not touched for a few years now, or so he'd told her in their meetings. But since he got money – her money – he'd started tanning it again, and was always stoned, lethargic.

The woman she'd seen him with the other night was always at his door now. At first, Emily had thought he had another woman on the go, but she'd quickly realised she was his dealer and she was a regular visitor to the flats. "Do I not make you happy anymore, John? Because something has changed with you lately. What happened to the man I first met? What happened to *Carpe Diem*?"

He slammed his palm on the sofa, and dust rose in the air. "Fuck me, don't start all that shit with me. I am who I am. I have good days and bad days. Maybe if you were here with me full-time, I wouldn't be like this. You mash my head up, woman."

"So, answer the question: do you still want me? Do you love me like you said you did? Because all I see at the moment is me giving you money and you sitting around smoking it all away."

John sprang to his feet, walking one way then the other. "Oh, how did I know you would make this about the money. You fucking rich bitches are all the same. Go on, fuck off home to your hubby and live your boring life."

Emily was fuming, though she didn't know if she was madder at John or at herself. She stood up. Enough was enough. There was no way she was having any man talking to her like that. "I was a fool thinking you would ever change. I've read through your paperwork time and time again and even that told me you were a high risk to re-offend. I should have never let you get under my skin. I'm an idiot, a bleeding idiot."

John let out a menacing laugh. "You wanted a bit of the rough stuff, love. Admit it, you thought you could save me, like the fucking do-gooder you are. I've sat about for long enough waiting for you to get your act together, but more fool me for listening to your bullshit. You love the sex I give you, love that I make you come like no man has before. So when you go on about giving me money, think about what you've been getting from me for free."

Emily went bright red, her eyes opened wide. "Who the hell do you think you are, talking to me like this? I've bankrolled your sorry arse for months, and all I've had in return is grief. You want me to leave my job, my girl, my fella for you, some washed-up tough guy who thinks the world owes him a favour. Go and get a bloody job like everyone else and stop thinking you're hard done to." Emily was on fire and at last she'd seen this man for who he really was. She could see now she'd been so grateful to him for saving her from Gavin Turner that she'd put up with everything since then, blinded to the truth.

John sat on the sofa and rolled a joint. He looked up at her and shook his head. "We're done. Yep, it's over. I can't be arsed with this anymore."

Emily felt like she'd woken from some kind of spell. She looked around the living room. It was a shit tip. Everywhere she looked were empty beer cans and cigarette packets. She'd had a lucky escape, she realised now.

Panic set in and she couldn't wait to get out of this place. "If it's over, don't come near me again. Don't phone me, don't contact me. I'll get your case transferred to another colleague and, with any luck, we'll never set eyes on each other again after..." John rolled the spliff about in his fingers and looked up at her. She had his attention and swallowed hard before she delivered her killer blow. "After you pay me back the money you owe me. I can't believe I let you get into my head to lend you so much money. Bloody hell, what a fool I've been." It was like a light had flicked on in her brain. "Get me out of this place," she whispered to herself. "Get me fucking out of here." She hooked her handbag over her shoulder and picked her way to the living room door, dodging his trainers left lying about.

John jumped up. "You think you can walk away from me just like that? No, no, no, Mrs. Expect me around at your house some time soon, because I'll be telling that husband of yours exactly what you've been doing. I think it's only fair, don't you, Emily? If you want me to pay, I think you should too."

She eyeballed him. "Do what you have to, wanker. If you think you can blackmail me, think again. I've wised up to what I want, and maybe it's not you *or* Archie."

John looked unbothered as he played his ace. "How do you think work would take it that you've been dating me, eh?"

Emily stood with her hand placed firmly on her hip. "I swear to you, John, if you so much as breathe one word to any of my colleagues, I'll ruin you. I'll make sure they bang you up in jail and throw away the key. You're forgetting what I know about you, forgetting that I know what you were planning and who you plotted to have over. You didn't think I was listening, but I was. Does the name Tony White ring any bells with you? You know, the one who lives on Collyhurst Village? I've looked up his file. Doesn't seem like the kind of guy who'd be pleased to hear how you were going to rip him over those guns."

John's face changed, and it was obvious she'd struck a nerve. He spoke through gritted teeth now. "Have it your way. Jena's your daughter, right? How would she feel if she knew exactly what her dirty mummy has been up to? I could show her some of your texts – horny little thing when you want to be, aren't you?"

"You stay the hell away from my daughter. I swear to you, if you go anywhere near her, I'll make sure you never breathe again. I know people who do stuff like that. My sister knows gangsters and people who will put you in a body bag for less than the money you've taken off me. So wind your neck in, John, and think about what you're saying before that big mouth of yours gets you into trouble."

John laughed out loud. "Where's all this street talk come from? You made out you were all posh and had high morals, but underneath it you're just the same as me."

But Emily didn't hang around to hear his speech. She left while she still could.

She sat in the car, sucking in long hard breaths. She opened the window to let fresh air in. Message alerts racked up on her phone, one, two, three. She didn't check them – she needed to be clear of this place first. She flicked the engine over and sped off, driving like a maniac.

She pulled onto her driveway and switched the engine off. She sat where she was, watching Archie walk about the lounge. Sure, he'd let her down in the past, but she'd done much worse now. How had she come so close to throwing all this away? The tears forced their way from her eyes. "I'm such a fool," she sobbed.

Archie came to the window and peered through. He would be waiting for her, kettle on, slippers ready for her the moment she walked through the front door. But how could she relax when she knew what John was threatening? She opened the car door and slowly walked towards the house. Archie opened the front door and she stood looking at him, her bottom lip trembling.

"Are you alright, love? You look in shock. What's up? Bad day at the office?"

Emily walked into the house with her head bowed, giving him no eye contact. "I'm fine, just not feeling like myself, that's all. I nearly made a big mistake at work – huge. I think I caught it in time, but it gave me a fright."

Archie watched her walk past him and went straight into the living room after her. "Come on, sit down and I'll make you a cuppa. I hate to see you upset like this.

Nothing is ever worth getting upset about. We can talk it out, make it all better." He went into the kitchen and shouted back, "You're going to love me, I've made tea. Chicken Bhuna. I found the recipe on the internet. Pretty easy really."

He came back into the lounge and placed a mug on the coffee table in front of Emily. Steam was circling from it and it was all she could look at. Archie sat next to her and said gently, "What's up, love? There is clearly something wrong, because I can tell you've been crying. Look at your eyes, they are red raw. Is it your mum playing on your mind? Because we can handle that." He reached across and bear-hugged her. Usually, Emily would have pulled away, but not today. She snuggled into his broad chest and inhaled deeply. Archie lifted her head to look into her eyes. "See, you're feeling better already, aren't you?"

Emily nodded. "Archie, I know things have not been good between us lately, but I do love you. I might not always show it, but we're a good match, aren't we?"

"Eh, come on now. Dry those tears and let's put this behind us. I love you too, and we've got through worse times than this. As long we're honest with each other, we can face anything."

She pulled away and shook her head. "Archie, I've—" But she was stopped dead in her tracks as Jena walked into the room. She had a face like thunder. Archie sat back and eyeballed his daughter. "Wow, what's up with your boat race? Lost a winning lottery ticket, or what?"

Jena was clearly in no mood for jokes. She was still in her pyjamas and her hair was tied up in a scruffy bun, but she looked more than just tired. Her eyes were dark-ringed and they looked bloodshot. "Teresa texted. Said she's on her way over. Apparently, she wants to talk to you about going to see my nana. If you two are going, I want to come too. I've missed out on having a grandmother all these years and now it looks like the only time I see her will be to say goodbye."

Archie looked pained. "What do you think, love? Is it time to face it?"

Emily was staring into space.

Jena shouted, clicking her fingers to bring her back to the present moment, "Hello, is anyone receiving?"

Emily surfaced from her trance. "I heard what you said. But I still don't know if I'm ready to go and see her. Lots of bad memories."

Jena sat down, pulled a cushion in front of her and hugged it with both arms. She looked ropey today, stressed. "Mam, come on, so what? Your mam had an affair, your dad's mate swung a punch or two. Yes, it's not great, but if your dad can get past it, surely you can. Water under the bridge and all that? My nana deserves a chance to put things right. And if she's ill, then if anything happens to her you will never forgive yourself if you haven't been to see her. It seems like time is not on your side."

"Don't go on at me about this. It's my decision and nobody else's. You two keep out of it. I'm not having this conversation with either of you, end of. You'll never know what it was like. She didn't only leave Dad, she left us. All three of us."

Jena stretched and looked out of the window. Well, here's Auntie Teresa. Maybe she can convince you."

Emily pulled her shoulders back and neatened her hair. She heard her sister's voice before she saw her. Teresa walked into the room with Jena following behind.

Teresa clocked that her sister had been crying. She pulled her coat off and passed it Archie. "Do us a favour, love, hang that up somewhere."

Archie slipped out of the room without a murmur. But Jena sat down again and tucked her legs under her. If there was any chance of getting gossip, she was there. "I've been telling my mam about you maybe going to see my nana. She's not listening to me. See if you can drum any sense into her."

Emily sighed and shook her head. "I've already told you this is none of your business. Go and get ready, and stop dossing about the house all day."

Jena rolled her eyes, but when it became clear she wasn't going to get any gossip, she jumped up and headed for the door.

Teresa said, "So, go on, why have you been crying? Don't say you haven't, because I can tell by the state of your eyes."

Emily sat upright and looked around the room. "Can we go out somewhere? I need to speak to you without wondering who can hear."

Teresa knew this wasn't a casual chat; this was a code red. She looked over at Emily's coffee and lowered her voice. "Right, but we can't just do one. I'll have to stay for ten minutes first. I'll say I'm taking you out for some fresh air."

"Anything, but get me out of here. Honestly, I feel like my head is going to explode."

Chapter Twenty-One

Shannon's eyes flickered: light, darkness. A pain pounding the side of her head. A smell she was familiar with filling her nostrils: stake tobacco, damp, misery. She moved her fingers slightly. A husky voice in her ear. "Wakey, wakey, my love. Daddy's home."

Her eyes opened wide, and fear took over every inch of her body. It was Paddy, right next to her, smiling at her. He stroked her head softly. "There, there, my girl. It's good to have you back home. I've been missing you. I'm not angry no more that you walked out on me. I'm just glad you are back home where you belong. Me and you back together, the dream team."

Shannon lay still, pain coursing through her. "Paddy, let me go. The police will be looking for me and they will come here first searching for me. You will end up in jail, on my life, they will throw away the key if you don't let me go."

His eyes changed, his voice too. "But I've thought of that. Nobody will find you again. I'm keeping you up here in the bedroom now. Here, I've got you some calming pills to help you sleep. You know I always look after you."

She shook her head. "I don't take them anymore. I'm clean, off any of the shit you rammed down my neck. Let me go, Paddy." She struggled to sit up, back pressed against the headboard. "I've told you, I'm done. I can't go back to how we were. I'm going to live with my mam and dad again until I get back on my feet."

Paddy gripped her by the throat, his eyes bulging with anger. "Oh, so you've got this all fucking mapped out, have you? No way. If you think you can walk out on me after all these years, you can think again."

"I'm over you, Paddy. You can beat me to death if you want but I still won't change my mind. You make my skin crawl. Look at you last night, pissed out of your head again. For years you have made me feel worthless. I will never feel like that again. I can start again, rebuild my life, find me."

"Stop talking out of your arse, woman. Whoever you've been listening to has filled your head with shit. You're a pill-popper, a slut who will sleep with anyone who gives you the time of day. I did you a favour by taking you on. What?" he paused. "Don't you think I heard all the stories about you? Fucking Yo-Yo Knickers, they called you behind your back, Shag-Bag Shannon. Here was me, like a dickhead, giving you a chance, and now you treat me like this. Take the tablets and have a sleep, then you can get back to normal. Like I said, I'm willing to overlook what's happened as long as it doesn't happen again."

She was dicing with death here; she should have stayed quiet and let him have his say. Kept her mouth shut. "Never. As soon as I get the chance, I will be gone from here. What, are you going to keep me locked away up here for the rest of my life? I would rather die than spend another second with you, Paddy, so do your –"

She'd not even finished the sentence before he backhanded her so hard she saw stars. "Slag, dirty fucking tramp. You will do as I tell you. Trust me, never again will you leave me."

Without warning, Shannon rolled onto her side and gripped his hair in her hands. This was what you called fighting for your life. She had no other choice. Despite all her injuries, something was spurring her on. She clawed at his eyes with her nails, biting him, punching him. She saw the lamp on the bedside cabinet was just in reach. She was nearly touching it, nearly had it in her grip, just a bit further. Paddy clocked what she was doing and went to town on her, punching into her ribs. Shannon let her arm fall away from the lamp; she was going nowhere anytime soon. Paddy let out a menacing laugh and headed to the bedroom door. "Nice to see you have a bit of fight in you. I like it rough."

Shannon cowered in the corner of the bed. The door slammed shut and she could hear his footsteps going down the stairs. She looked about the bedroom – her prison, even smaller than before. Already it felt like her time outside of here had been a dream. She cried tears of sadness and fear, tears of not knowing how long this nightmare would last.

Chapter Twenty-Two

Archie sat down and opened a can of lager. Well, Emily was out and the footy was on. He took a large mouthful from the can and took the horizontal position on the sofa. Manchester United had been his life when he was growing up. He'd followed them since he was a child. His family were all reds, and he lived and breathed football. Sometimes he wished he'd got Jena into it so he had someone to watch the match with. Instead, he gave himself a running commentary. "Fucking hell, where is Rashford? Surely, you've not got him as sub?"

There was knocking at the front door. He kept his eyes on the TV, hoping whoever it was would piss off and leave him to watch the football. Knocking again. "For crying out loud, do these fucking idiots not know the bleeding footy is on?" he moaned as he walked into the hallway. If this was bloody double-glazing reps again, they were getting told. He yanked the door open. How many times did they need telling he wasn't interested in any new windows? But Archie stared at the man stood there, speechless.

At last, he held his hand out to Sam. "Bleeding hell, mate, you were the last person I expected to see at my front door. Come in out of the cold. Emily's out. There is only me in. You're not going to credit it, but she's actually out with Teresa. They're making up for lost time, I think. I wish you'd said you were coming. I would have made sure they were both here."

"I'm staying here until they do come home, pal. Sick of pussyfooting around. I'm their father and I need to speak to them. Their mother is lying in bed at home, terminally ill. I've sent letters to them all but time's running out. I know the way things fell apart at home isn't easy to forgive, but Brenda needs her girls one last time. And more's the point, I think the girls need it too. You've tried your best over the years to talk with Emily but she's a bloody stubborn cow."

Archie sighed, still shooting his eyes over to the TV, making sure not to miss any goals. "Park yourself there, Sam. I'll grab you a can and you can watch the match with me. At least when they get back, you will get the both of them. Kill two birds with one stone."

"So, Teresa is here too, since when?" Sam was relieved.

"A few weeks now, pal. She's had a bit of a hard time by the looks of her, and she's moved back down to our ends to sort herself out. I don't know if it's man trouble or money worries. You know what Emily's like. She tells me sod all, only what she wants to tell me. She's been acting strange too."

Archie passed Sam a can. "Get that cold one down your neck."

Sam looked around the living room. He'd not been here in many years, and his eyes filled up as he spotted a school photo on the wall. "Look at her there. Look at all three of them, they look so happy. Family means everything, until it falls apart – rips you open, it does."

Sam pointed to a photo of his granddaughter now. "Where is Jena, is she home? It's not just Brenda. *I've* missed out on so much because of this feud. We all have. None of us are innocent in all this, are we?"

Archie replied quickly. "Jena's out too. She's another one who I don't know if I'm coming or going with. Hormonal, maybe. She's all grown up but sulks like a kid if you ask her anything about where she's going or who with. Women, eh? A bloody mystery. Can't live with em, can't live without em." Archie realised too late what he'd said and saw in his father-in-law's face that he couldn't hold the tears back. "How am I ever going to live without my Brenda? I can't even think about it."

"Come on mate, Brenda is a fighter. She will hold on as long as she can."

Sam stared at the floor. "I want my family together one time – and while I've still got my Bren, not at her funeral when it's too late. I know things happened in the past, but we've got a chance to draw a line under that. She's got things she needs to say to them – big things. We've all sinned, and now it's time to ask forgiveness."

Archie went bright red, paranoid that Sam was referring to him. "I'm with you, Sam. When your letter came, I was in your corner for sure, and Jena was too. She told her mum how much she had missed out on with you and Bren. After all, you're still her grandparents, no matter what. You've missed a lot of years with her."

"We sure have. I was the one who helped you both out when all that stuff happened years ago, but old scars still ache, I know that much."

Archie gulped and his eyes opened wide, small balls of sweat forming on his forehead. This was a road he didn't want to go down; his infidelity was something that belonged firmly in the past. His voice was low as he replied. "All we can do is speak to Emily and hope she listens. You know what your Teresa is like. She'll make up her own mind and there'll be no changing it."

"The girls have always been strong, Archie. Putting up with what they did makes or breaks you, you know – and I feel so guilty that those girls had to raise themselves. They thought they'd seen me killed in front of them, and I'm not lying when I tell you, sometimes I think it might have been better for them if I had never got up again. True, they got their dad back, but I was no father to them for years. I was a broken man and they had to get by any way they could. You know Shannon is the only one who has come to see us. I thought she was the one damaged the most – but she's the one who's answered the letter. She's sat with her mam for hours talking and straightening out the past."

The colour drained from Archie's face, and he stood up. "Just going to the lav." He walked out. He needed time to think, now his past and present were colliding.

Across town, Jena stood in a corner ,watching the clubbers, music pumping in her ears, baseline in her throat. She was extra vigilant tonight. The texts she'd received told her she was being watched and she was a dead man walking if her debt was not paid in full. She'd been stupid to think she could skim a bit off the top. Maybe she could talk to the dealers, tell them she could make it right – if they could just give her some more time. If she started selling at better places, she knew she could make more money. She walked into the toilets and nodded at two girls. A small package was passed, some notes given back. Jena went inside a cubicle and rammed the money into her bra. She pulled out a small bag of white powder and stared at it. She'd promised Teresa she wouldn't touch the stuff again, but she couldn't stop just like that, she would have to wean herself off it. She tapped the white powder onto the toilet seat and snorted the two lines. She stood tall, head held against the toilet door as she felt the rush from the cocaine surging through her body. She closed her eyes and felt her anxiety drain away. It was game on now; she would be on the ball, confident, the life and soul of the party. As she walked out of the toilets, she barged past a gang of men who leered at her, reaching out, touching her, trying to grope her tits. Normally she'd have just walked off but right now she felt like she could take on the world.

Her eyes bulged as she went nose-to-nose with one of them. "Off the cloth, moth. Don't touch me. I'm not here for the taking. Have a bit of respect, eh?"

The man wasn't happy being shown up in front of his mates. He held his arm against the wall, blocking her path.

"Listen, you fucking coke-whore, wind your neck in and fuck off. In fact," his hand went deep into her pocket knowing what she would be carrying, "I'll be having these for my trouble. Do one. Fuck off out of my face before I call that bouncer over there," he jerked his head. "You say a word and I'll be telling him you've been supplying drugs on his watch."

The rush of the lines had worn off and Jena felt her heart racing. "Give me the sniff back and I'll be on my way. It's not my drugs, I'm just passing it on. Please," she pleaded.

"Nah, daft bitch, move out of my face. That's the thing with you girls these days, you think you can chat shit to us guys."

Jena knew she was in trouble. This guy wouldn't think twice about banging her out, putting her on the floor. She'd met his sort before, and he had wife-beater written all over him. She swallowed hard as she edged away from him. This was a nightmare – no drugs, no money to be earned, and her debt racking up. She would have earned four or five hundred quid tonight off that amount. Her head was in bits as she walked across the dance floor, looking behind her, aware she was a sitting duck with no friends to have her back. Every second she was in this club her life was in danger. If any of her supplier's contacts had seen her get done over, they could attack at any second. With speed in her step, she headed straight out of the club, not even breathing out until she was past security on the door. Once outside, she scurried to the side of the club, watching for anyone who might be following her. She was being paranoid, but she was better safe than sorry. She pulled out a cigarette and sparked it up. She had some big decisions to make – should she run, or stand and face what was waiting for her? The clock was ticking, and she needed to sort her head out before the choice was taken away from her.

Chapter Twenty-Three

Emily sat with her head in her hands, waiting for Teresa to come back from the bar with the drinks. How had she let herself get into a situation like this? She should have known better – she should have listened to Teresa. This was her third drink and she was knocking them back like nobody's business. She glanced around the pub, looking for John. He should have been here an hour ago. Cheeky bastard, making her wait. Teresa had rung him and arranged this meeting. Hopefully they could all sit down like adults, and walk away from this with no casualties. John had been a cocky fucker on the phone too, full of himself, Teresa said.

Teresa was back now, and slapped her wrist. "Stop biting your nails, woman. There will be nothing left of them if you carry on like that. I've told you, when he comes, I'll be the one doing the talking. You sit there and keep quiet. I've dealt with dickheads like him every day. I'll knock him down a peg or two if he thinks he's pulling a fast one on you. Hold your tongue and, no matter what he throws at you, keep calm. This is like a game of poker, and he will be watching your face for any sign of weakness. If all else fails, I have a plan B up my sleeve. Not something I want to put into play but, if the shit hits the fan, I'll have no other option."

Emily was flustered. "I can't thank you enough for doing this. You were right. It was madness – and it's not only the money. I could lose my job, my marriage, the bleeding lot."

Teresa rolled her eyes. "I'm not going to say I told you so, because it's pointless. You did what you did and, if we play our cards right here tonight, this fella will walk away when we're done, and you will never hear from him again. But, trust me, he's out to line his pockets. You're giving him nothing more than what you've paid out already. Not another penny, do you hear me? I don't care what he threatens to do, you hold your own and agree to zilch." Teresa checked her wristwatch again and shot a look around the boozer. It was empty tonight. Only the men's darts team playing a match at the other side of the pub, shouting, bantering, laughing at one another.

Emily nudged her sister, nodding over at the door. "He's here. Oh, for crying out loud, I think I'm having a panic attack. Breathe woman, bloody breathe and get your act together," she told herself.

Teresa glared at her sister. "Sort yourself out, you're doing my head in. Even when you were a young girl you were the bloody same, always flapping and thinking the worst. For once, pull them shoulders back and play the fucking game."

That was Emily told and the bollocking seemed to work because now she was sat up straight with steady eyes. She was ready to rumble.

John clocked the two of them sat in the corner of the boozer and went straight to the bar to grab a pint. Emily watched him. She wanted to run at him and scratch his eyes out. How could what they had have turned to this in the blink of an eye? She realised now she had been a sitting duck for him – a middle-aged woman, overlooked, ready for someone to shake up her world. She was a fool for believing a word of it. Had it all been one big lie? The sex had felt so right – but was even that put on, a chore for him? Was he running other women at the same time, she wondered now? Probably that blonde lady she'd seen him with. He'd told Emily she supplied him with weed, but Emily could have bet her bottom dollar he was sleeping with her.

"Brace yourself. Showtime," Teresa whispered.

John bounced towards them and slammed his pint down on the table. He sat next to Emily and patted his cold hand on her knee. Full of himself, he was. "Looking a bit rough, Em. Something on your mind?"

What an arsehole. Did he not have any shame? Emily peeled his fingers from her leg and sneered at him. She was about to give him a mouthful when Teresa chirped in. "Right, I'll cut the bullshit and get straight to the point, shall I?"

John sat back in his seat and nodded. "Yep, crack on. I'm all ears."

Teresa licked her lips and took a mouthful of her red wine. She had to play this cool, let this prick know he was not messing with a couple of idiots. She placed her glass down slowly on the table and looked him directly in the eyes. "OK, so let's get this lot out on the table. You two were involved with each other and it never worked out. Sad story, but it doesn't mean you have to burn everything down, does it?"

John let out a sarcastic laugh. "She fed me a load of crap, telling me she was leaving her husband. But it was all bollocks. Used me, she did."

Emily snapped, pointing her finger at him, "You knew I was married. I told you that from the start and you said it wasn't a problem. You chased me. The long and short of this story is that you owe me money and I want it back, every bastard penny. You never loved me, you only wanted to fleece me, you bent bastard." Emily had promised to be quiet, let her sister do the talking, but she was in the zone now. "Go on, tell Teresa what you told me – that you were coming to see Archie and Jena to tell them about our fling. Tell her you said you would come to my work and tell them too. Wanker," she hissed.

John answered slowly, cool as cucumber. He knew the dance and made sure they both could hear everything he had to say. "The way I see it is that I'm the one who is hard done to, here. Taken advantage of by the person who was meant to be helping me go straight. I'm the one who's had my heart broken, the one who has been lying in bed each night on my tod waiting for Emily to pluck up the courage to tell her husband she was leaving him. Go on, you did say you were binning him. You told me he couldn't fulfil you in the bedroom like I can."

Emily went beetroot. How dare he shout out what happened in the bedroom.

Teresa stepped in: this was too much information. "So, is that your plan to ruin the woman you said you loved?"

"It is what it is, isn't it. Life's a bitch sometimes."

"What do you want? Fuck going around the houses, we're all adults here. Put it out there – what are you hoping to gain from all this?"

John sat playing with his fingers, cracking his knuckles, thinking. "I want the rest of the ten grand, money to help me move on. I put my life on the line to get it back from that psycho, Gavin. I think I've earned it."

Emily nearly choked. "You can get to fuck. Over my dead body are you getting another single penny out of me."

Teresa shook her head. "I really thought you were a decent guy, John," she lied. "If you loved my sister like you said you did, surely you wouldn't put her through any more misery. Shit happens and it's not worked out for you both. Yes, you put your neck on the line for her, and don't think we're not grateful. But you've had two grand for it. Not bad for a morning's work. Can you not both shake hands and walk away as friends?"

"Five grand, and I fuck off," said John. "Seems fair we split it, considering we shared everything else." He winked.

It was the wink that sent Emily over the edge. "Five Gs? Do you know how many years it's taken me to build that nest egg? You think I'm rich, working in the parole office? I've given that job the best years of my life and, now I finally have a little safety net, you think you can pull it from under me? I'll tell you now, you're getting not another penny from me. So, if that's how you want to play it, off you trot. Go and see Archie and tell him everything. It will save me a job. And as for telling work about our fling, off you go there too. I'll tell them you're lying, because who will they listen to – a trusted colleague, or some ex-con dodgy fucker with a vendetta? I'll tell them you nicked my phone – sent yourself those texts. Then you have no proof, none whatsoever. I'll tell them you had a thing for me, made a few remarks in our meetings. I'll do my best to have you banged back in jail. And you know I can." This was a woman on a mission, and she wasn't finished either. "We've offered you a good deal here. If you won't listen to us, I'll give that bloke down Collyhurst a call so he knows what a snake you are. It'll be easy too. Did you know he's on probation with another team? He doesn't sound like the kind of guy who'd take kindly to being done over for some unregistered guns."

John was upright in his seat now, listening carefully, nostrils flaring.

Teresa was aware people were looking over "Oi, you two, do you want the world and his wife to know all your business, or what? Keep your voices down."

"I don't give a fuck who's listening. Mrs fucking Fancy Pants here thinks she can have me over. You're just a desperate old hag who wanted a bit of fresh meat, someone to make you feel good about your boring pathetic life. Do you know what?" He looked around him and kept his voice low. "It was like grab-a-granny shagging you, anyway. You should have been paying me for having sex with you, you cheeky cow. You can ask you sister here what her rates are, eh?" He stood up, placed one hand in his jeans pocket and licked his front teeth. "I'll be around at your gaff sometime in the near future. I'll tell your husband just how much you screamed my name when I was inside you."

Emily lost it, reached over and sank her fingers into his eyes. "Bastard!"

Teresa split them up and stood in front of her sister. John was ready to go for her, but she stood tall and never flinched.

"You'll have to go through me first, love, if you want to get to her. You're a scumbag and you're lucky my sister even gave you the time of the day. Look at you, scruffy twat. Go back home to your sad little gaff. And, for the record, remember the man you done in for me? He's an ex of mine and I'm sure he would love a little anonymous tip-off about your name and where you live."

John was already walking away, aware this round was over. Emily grabbed the pint pot from the table, ready to launch it at the back of his head.

Teresa got to her just in time. "What the hell are you doing? Put that down. The last thing you need on your plate is a charge sheet."

Emily fell back on her chair, her emotions taking over.

The landlord was on his way over and it was left to Teresa to sort him out. "I'm so sorry about the noise. It was a misunderstanding. It's all sorted now."

The landlord sighed. "I run a nice respectable place. I don't have none of that shouting and screaming going on in here. In future, leave the domestics at home, will you?"

"Yes. It won't happen again."

Emily wasn't even looking at the landlord, she was searching in her bag for a tissue. The tears were flowing now and her mascara drew dark trails down her face.

Suddenly there was a loud bang and shards of glass shattered everywhere. Someone had launched a brick through the window near where they sat. Teresa gripped her big sister by the arm. The police would be here soon, and they could do without giving a statement. The landlord was yelling and punters were running about the pub, trying to see what had happened. Teresa looked one way, then the other, and dragged Emily out of the boozer amid the commotion.

"It must have been John," Emily sobbed as they scarpered. "He's never going to let it lie, is he? Maybe I should go and report him to the police? I'll lose my job but at least I might be safe that way. He's tapped in the head, a nutter."

"You're doing nothing. Let's get away from here, then I can think straight. Him lobbing a brick shows he's desperate, not some criminal mastermind."

Emily was struggling to run, panting like a dog on a hot summer's day. She stopped near an old building at the end of the street. "I'm going to have a bleeding-heart attack. Let me catch my breath. Honest, I'm seeing double now, I'm going to keel over."

Teresa scouted the area and made sure they were not being followed. She hid away in the shadows and sat down in the entrance to a deserted warehouse. The putrid smell made her retch.

Emily paced up and down, kicking at things on the floor, talking to herself. "He won't get the better of me, no bloody way in this world. Oh my God, Teresa, how could I have been so thick? I feel so ashamed. You were right. But perhaps John was right too: I've been a desperate woman adjusting to feeling invisible and looking for some attention. Archie doesn't deserve this. He can never find out. It would break him."

Teresa spoke without thinking. "Not like *he* can talk, is it? You owed him, in my eyes, and if all this comes out, remind him about when *he* was caught with his pants down."

Emily's bottom lip trembled. She stood with her back to the wall. "How could I ever forget his affair? I'm constantly reminded every single day. I know you looked at me at the time and thought I was off my rocker, but I needed a child, needed to be a mother. Do you know how it feels to be told you will never have children?"

Teresa came to her sister's side and patted her shoulder. "No love, I can't say I'm the maternal type. You know my son's living with his dad, so I can't say a word about anybody's parenting skills. It should have been me who was unable to have children, not you."

Emily looked into the night sky and twiddled a piece of hair that had fallen onto her face. "I thought about having a baby every single day, looked at them in prams or on the TV, felt a constant ache in my heart. When Archie had the one-night-stand and we found out she was pregnant, it made sense for us to have the baby. She could never have looked after her like we could, she told us that herself. We went through all those years of IVF and the doctor had told me I was wasting my money. We had even talked about finding a surrogate, so I felt it saved us a job. But my own kid sister? I should have known I'd never be able to put it behind me. Jena is just like her, isn't she? She smiles like her, rolls her eyes like her too."

"I don't know how you ever forgave her." Teresa frowned.

"I forgave her, but I didn't ever forget. Yes, she broke my heart, but she also gave me the chance to be a mother."

"Will you ever tell Jena, Emily? I've thought about this a lot. You know what Shannon's like. Even though she said she would take the secret to the grave, it only takes her getting twisted and she could blurt it out."

Emily wiped at the wet patches on her cheeks. "I've got to admit I was relieved when Shannon stopped getting in touch. I stopped having to pretend everything was OK. But this letter from Dad has had me on the edge again. If we go to see Mum, Jena says she wants to come. What if she sees Shannon and notices they're the spit of each other? It's the kind of thing that might make anyone ask questions."

"You're safe there, Em. Jena takes after Archie most of all. Still, I don't trust Shannon not to crumble if she's back home, back where it all happened. I remember, when we were still in touch, she lost the plot once when I told her I was sending our Joel to live with his dad. Said no real mother would give up her child without a fight. There was a look in her eyes that told me she'd never let this lie. Maybe it's time we settled this – once and for all."

Chapter Twenty-Four

Teresa left Emily at the end of her street. She kissed her on the cheek and hugged her tightly. "I've got to get a few things sorted. If John is willing to go all the way with this, like he's threatened, then we need a back-up plan."

"But where are you going? You need to tell me so I know you're safe." Emily was flustered. "I don't want you getting into more crap because of me. I'd rather go into the house now and tell Archie everything. This is my shit, and I need to step up and take responsibility for my actions."

"You do nothing. I know I can stop this going any further. It might cost me, but at least we will all have peace. Go home and wait til I call. I'll be back when I've sorted stuff out. Give me a few days, though; don't be flapping if I'm not back. I'm a big girl and I can look after myself. When I am back, we'll go to Mum and Dad's together. Face it all."

Emily's bottom lip trembled. "I thought I was a big girl too, but look at me, I'm a walking wreck. Teresa," she paused. "I'm meant to be your big sister but you're the one looking after me. I know we have not been that close for a long time and I'm sorry for not making more of an effort."

Teresa hugged her again. "I know, but eh, shit happens, and I'm as much to blame as you. I could have made more of an effort and rang you. There were too many skeletons in the cupboard for us all to play happy families. At least now, we've been honest about who we are, the mistakes we've made. We can only look at the future now and fix what was broken. Anyway, we've been bleeding stood here for over ten minutes. It's the longest goodbye ever," she chuckled. "See you soon, and straighten that face before you go into the house. I'll sort this, I've got your back." Teresa turned and walked away. Her car was parked over the road and, as she neared it, her pace quickened. Trouble like this didn't sort itself out – it took someone like her to get it sorted.

Emily's hand shook as she placed her key into the front door. Teresa was right, she could simply go inside and pretend everything in the garden was rosy; she'd been doing it for years anyway, pretending her marriage was perfect. She stepped inside and could feel the warmth straight away. It hugged her like an old friend and made her feel safe. She kicked her shoes off and shouted into the lounge, "It's only me, Archie. Bang that kettle on, will you? I'm just going to put my pyjamas on, and I'll be back down." She ran up the stairs and went straight into her bedroom. Quickly, she yanked her clothes off and grabbed a pair of pale-blue pyjamas from the bed. She tied her hair up, and she was ready to go back downstairs. As she walked along the landing, she popped her head inside her daughter's bedroom. It was a weekday and Jena was usually in bed at this time, watching a film on Netflix. She stomped downstairs and walked into the lounge–

"Dad!" she spluttered.

Sam stood up. There was no need for words, the hug said it all.

"Dad, what are you doing here?" Emily finally asked. "Don't tell me she's passed away. I was going to come, I meant to ring you, but I've had so much on my plate lately. Please don't tell me she's gone; I wouldn't be able to take it."

Emily sat down and Sam sat next to her, still holding her hand. The same hand he used to hold on the way to school, the same hand he held when she had fallen over. "I should have come sooner – your mam's clinging on, but she wants to speak with you. She knows she did wrong, but so did I. After she left, my head was in bits, and I wasn't in a good place. There is a lot more to the story that you don't know about. I'm as much to blame as she is for our family falling apart."

Emily screwed her face up. "Dad, that guy she was sleeping with left you for dead and my mam didn't care, about you or her kids. She never thought about any of us when she started having the affair. She hurt us all, every one of us." Emily stopped. Who was she to judge her mother now she had done more or less the same thing? Emily hadn't cared about her family when she was in the arms of another man, had she?

Sam closed his eyes for a second to gather his thoughts. "Like I said, you don't know the full story."

"So, tell me. Help me understand."

"We had been married for years and, back then, I liked a few beers every Friday night down the boozer with the lads. Most men went down the pub on Fridays after a hard day's graft, it was just a given. The barmaid in the Hat and Feathers was a great-looking woman and all the men were always trying to bed her. I never did. I was a married man and she never interested me." Sam took a swig from his can of beer. "Anyway, I'd had a few too many one night and Carol was all over me. I couldn't believe my luck; all the men were jealous of me and couldn't understand it. I was flattered too. She gave me confidence, made me feel good about myself. It doesn't sound too clever, I know, but it just happened. I slept with her after walking her home one night. I hated myself afterwards. I was guilt-ridden for weeks. But I couldn't stop thinking about her. Your mam was at home looking after you lot and, if I'm being honest, she never really had time for me anymore. She was always tired, moaning about not having enough money, and we hadn't slept together for months."

Emily leaned in and urged him to continue.

"Before I knew it, I was spending more and more time with Carol and we both got to the stage where we were falling in love. She gave me an ultimatum: she wanted us to be together, to live together, to have a life with each other."

Emily shook her head. This was all news to her. It was a mirror-image of her life. She was more like her father than she cared to admit.

"I came home and told your mother the truth, told her about Carol, and I started to pack my belongings. She begged me to stay, you know. Cried on her knees, asking me not to leave her, telling me she would change, do anything it took to save our marriage. I just walked out, Emily, never listened to a word she said, left her heartbroken."

This was serious news. Emily was quiet, digesting everything she'd just been told. Her poor mother, a young baby, left on her own, her husband running off with a tart from the local boozer. She must have been out of her mind. Emily couldn't look at her dad. In her eyes, he'd always been the perfect husband who waited on her mother hand and foot.

Sam finished off his story. "The new relationship lasted about two months. Carol was still working in the pub and my mates were telling me she was still the local bike in there. I told her there was no way I was having her working behind the bar anymore, and it all went south from there. I woke up one morning and realised what I had done. I went straight back to your mother and begged and begged her to have me back. Honest, I would sit outside the front door all night long, sobbing my heart out, crying to her through the letter box."

Emily pulled her shoulders back and sucked hard on her gums. "And so you bloody should. She must have been out of her mind with it all."

"She was, love. I had broken her in two and, when she finally let me in to speak to her, I could see with my own two eyes how much I had hurt her. She was as thin as a rake, smoking like a chimney and she couldn't look me in the eye. She said I made her stomach churn, made her feel sick."

Emily could relate to that feeling. Even now, just talking about someone cheating on their partner, that same feeling came flooding back into her body. She rubbed at her arms, felt a cold chill climbing up her spine.

"So, now you know the truth, you know why she slept with my best friend a few years later when the opportunity knocked. And, more than anything, you now know why I couldn't take the higher ground when it was me who struck the first blow."

Emily couldn't believe how history was repeating itself. "I know how it feels, Dad, when an affair is uncovered. It ruins you from head to toe. It took me years to even look at Archie again and I had Jena to remind me every day of what he had done."

"I know, love, I know. What you did to raise Jena took grit. I don't know a lot of people who would have done what you did. I told Shannon that too. I know she said she wanted to keep the baby, but she was in no fit state to be a mother at that age. She was smoking pot and taking God knows what other drugs. She blames me, you know; I can see it in her eyes."

"Shannon was wild, Dad. Archie was the one to blame. He crossed the line when he slept with my sister. If it wasn't for the baby, I'd have binned him."

Emily looked down at her hands, at her wedding ring. The circle of trust, she used to call it. The ring looked dull, the shine gone from it years ago. She twisted it around slowly and remembered throwing it at Archie's face when his affair was uncovered. She closed her eyes and could see that night fresh in her mind again: the noises from behind the toilet door, her sister laughing. They both said it was just the once, a drunken fumble when both of them were pissed. But was it only once? All men say it was only once when they get caught with their pants down, didn't they? No one ever really knew the truth, bar the two involved.

Emily looked at her father in more detail. He was older than she remembered: deep wrinkles, dark circles under his eyes, lack of sleep. "Dad, I'll come over first thing in the morning. I'll bring Teresa with me. I've been with her tonight, but she had to rush off to go and see somebody."

Sam looked relieved. "I said to your mother you would all come, told her it wasn't too late. But I need to get going, love. If you come and see your mam tomorrow, I know she will be able to rest. Since they told her the cancer would never leave her body, all she's ever spoken about is her girls. Said she would not be going anywhere until she's fixed everything she's broken."

"Will Shannon be there?" Emily needed to prepare herself.

Sam nodded. "Yes, she came and stayed all day with her – said she'd be back tomorrow. She's had a hard time lately. She has been staying at a women's refuge, she said. That boyfriend of hers knocked her about, made her life a misery. I hope she's coming back to live with us."

Archie came in now and draped his arm around Emily's shoulder. They both walked Sam to the door and watched him get into his car and drive away.

Archie looked at Emily and smiled. "Maybe this is it – we're finally laying ghosts to rest."

Emily was already walking back into the lounge. "Where did Jena say she was going?"

"Not got a clue, she just said see you later."

Emily felt a strong urge to keep her family close. Too many secrets were swirling around, and Jena was at a vulnerable age.

Archie could tell she was ready for breaking. "Come here, love, don't be getting upset. It's all going to be sorted out tomorrow and you will feel like a weight has been lifted from you."

Emily looked deep into her husband eyes. "I hope you're right, Archie, I hope you're right."

Chapter Twenty-Five

Teresa walked into the nightclub and scanned the place. The base was pumping, drilling her ears. Usually, she might have had a bit of a boogie on the dance floor, but not tonight. No, she had to keep focused. Gavin would be in here somewhere and she had to find him before he found her. She was dicing with death coming back to Burnley, and she knew this could all go wrong at the drop of a hat.

Bingo! Over to the left she clocked him sat with his cronies. He always sat team-handed, never alone, always protected. She patted her jacket pocket and slowly moved towards him. All eyes were on her now. One of the men stood up and tried to grip her by the arm, but she shrugged him off. "Piss off, Jonah. I'm here of my own free will, so take your stupid fat hands from me, you dickhead."

Gavin sat back in his chair and nodded. "Cheeky bitch, aren't you, walking in here like I won't end your fucking life?"

She looked at the other men and flicked her hair back over her shoulder. She had to hold it together, keep her cool. "If you let me speak to you in private, I will explain everything. I've got the money I owe you, so you can relax."

Gavin rubbed his hands together. This was music to his ears. "Come and sit down here, next to me, and let's see it, then. You are lucky you weren't at home when I called. Your sister is lucky too, because I would have ended her, on my life. A body bag she was going in until that goon of hers rocked up."

Teresa waited for the men to stand up and she edged past them, watching her back, making sure she was on guard in case they one-bombed her. "Do one, guys, and let me have five minutes with this one," he shouted over to his boys.

Teresa was sat next to him now. His aftershave surrounded her like a cloud. Gavin had always smelt good, smelt of money, power. He turned and faced her, licking his lips. "So, let's hear it. In fact, before we go any further, flash that cash, then I can relax."

Teresa reached inside her pocket and pulled out a brown envelope. "It's all there, every penny. I told you I was good for it. I just needed a bit of extra time, so I've put a bit of interest in there too."

Gavin was impressed and lifted the flap on the envelope, checking there was really cash in there.

"Impressed, Teresa. I thought you had sold me out. In fact, there is money on your head, as we speak. I better call it off. A few grand they wanted to take you down. You see how cheap I get things for?"

Teresa stayed cool. "So get on the blower and call the hit off. I'm not moving from here until you do. Your lads are bleeding head-the-balls and wouldn't think twice about popping a cap in me to earn a few quid."

"Chill, woman, I'll sort it, hold on a second." Gavin pulled his mobile phone out and made a call. It was as easy as that. The hit was cancelled.

Teresa was relieved, glad she'd made the decision to come back and face her demons. It hurt handing over such a chunk of cash – but it was safer to owe Teddy than Gavin, she admitted to herself. "Gav, I know I'm not your favourite person at the moment, but I need a big favour."

He burst out laughing. "You see, that's why I like you. You have more front than Blackpool. Nothing stops you."

She giggled and playfully punched him in the arm. "We were good together once, Gavin. We had some good times, didn't we?"

He smirked and nodded, looking her up and down. "We did and we can again, if you are up for it. You understand me, know my shit, know the world I ride in. You see, all these other women, they peck my head, always wanting to know where I am, who I have been talking to. No trust. Whereas you, yep, you are chilled and laid back. But," he paused. "You're a brass, Teresa. I could never have a woman who sells her body on my arm full-time."

"You're a cheeky bastard, Gavin. I am a businesswoman, just like you. You sell drugs and guns and whatever else you sell. Whereas me, I sell happiness."

He took a mouthful of his beer. "So, go on, spill. What do you want from me?"

She edged closer. "You know that guy who was at my house when you came, the one who put you on your arse?"

He didn't let her get another word out. "That twat got lucky, stole one on me when I wasn't looking. I swear, I'm already doing my homework on him and, when I get his name, the prick will be dealt with. I'm going to torture him for what he did to me. I was in a bad way, proper fucked up."

Teresa kept her voice steady. "I can save you the leg work. That's why I am here. That snake is bad news and he's trying to have my sister over. To cut a long story short, my sister was sleeping with him and he's threatening to tell her husband, ruin her, wreck her life. I need him gone, out of the picture, and you say you was already gunning for him, so it's a no-brainer."

Gavin stared around the club, thinking. "Consider it done. You give me that cunt's name and where his yard is, and I will do the rest. You know what? Hats off to you for coming back and facing me. That takes balls and I like that in a woman. You could have hidden away for years and had me over for the money, but you came back, and that goes down well in my books, that does. We're all straight now after this." He leaned in and kissed her.

Teresa let him, though she still had one eye open – this man was dangerous, and she wasn't looking to get back into anything heavy. If you lived by the sword, you died by it, and she didn't fancy meeting her maker just yet. Teresa pulled away and smiled at him. "Let's have a night together and see if we still have chemistry."

Gavin grinned. "I'm up for that. After all, I like to try before I buy, if you get what I mean?" He gave her a cheeky wink.

Later that night, Teresa looked over at Gavin in the bed, dead to the world. Was she making a big mistake getting involved with him again? But, what else did she have on the go? Gavin was her meal ticket and, if she used her head wisely, she could get back on her feet and live the life she was accustomed to. She stroked a finger up and down his chest. He moaned a little and rolled on his side. She could rebuild her life with him, go on nice holidays, have nice handbags, jewellery. Who was she kidding thinking she'd settle for a quiet life somewhere?

Chapter Twenty-Six

Emily held her breath and read the text message from her sister.

"Home soon, stop worrying, just sorting a few things out in my old gaff. Love T."

She placed her mobile next to her on the sofa and carried on watching the television. Still, she jumped at the slightest noise, froze every time the telephone rang. She was constantly on edge – waiting for another brick through the window, or worse, John at the door.

Archie walked in and shook his head, sick to death of his wife living on her nerves.

"I'm worried sick about Jena. I've tried ringing her phone but she's still not answering. I'll strangle her when I get my hands on her, having me worrying like this. She knows what I'm like, why is she so selfish? How hard is one phone call to let me know she's safe?"

"You worry too much, love." Archie went into the kitchen, and she could hear him whistling. He was such a cheery chappy, she wished she could be as carefree as he was. Archie came back, humming a song. She shook her head and smiled to herself. Like a bleeding budgie, he was, whistling and singing.

"So, where is Teresa? I thought she was going to come back with you last night?"

Emily swallowed hard and started playing with her hair, twisting and turning it. She didn't look at him. "She was going to, but an old friend rang her, and she said she was going to meet up with them and go straight back to her hotel. But I'll see her at our folks' – if she shows up. It's all such a bleeding mess, Arch. I can't even think straight. Work is doing my head in, and all." She let out a breath. "It's just one thing after another, lately."

"What's up at work? Why don't you change jobs if it makes you feel like that? I've always thought you were overqualified for that job, anyway."

"I might start looking and see what is out there." Emily felt lighter at the thought.

"Do what makes you happy, love. You only get one life, so you have to make the most of it. This isn't a test run, it's the real shit."

Emily started to calm down and hugged a cushion on her lap. "Archie, what will I even say to my mam when I get there? What my dad told me has put a new spin on everything – but it doesn't make it all OK. What happened to us girls, what happened with Shannon and Jena. All those secrets don't simply melt away because my mum's on her last legs."

"Do you want me to come with you, you know, a bit of support?"

"No, I need a bit of space to do this. No point in putting it off anymore, is there? I'm going over tomorrow, whether or not Teresa or Shannon are there. I'm finally facing it all."

It was mid-morning the following day by the time Emily sat outside her parents' home. It was just how she remembered it. Even the blinds on the windows were the same. She turned the engine off and grabbed her black leather handbag. Deep breaths, one two three. She opened the car door and hooked her handbag over her shoulder. Her heart was pounding with every step she took. No sooner had she closed the garden gate than her dad was stood at the front door with a smile on his face. He must have been at the window all morning, waiting for her.

"I'm so happy you've come, Emily. Come on, get inside and I'll bang the kettle on."

Emily walked down the hallway and straight into the living room. Her childhood came flooding back to her. Laughter, running about the house being chased by her sisters, the games they played, the happy times in this house, all flooding her memory. And then the darker things – seeing her dad bleeding out on the front path, the years of neglect that followed. And then, when she thought she'd escaped the place, moved out and got married young, she'd been pulled back when Shannon dropped her bombshell. It was here, in the front room, that her dad had made Shannon tell her sister what had happened. Here that she'd seen Shannon's pregnant stomach and not been able to believe it was Archie's child. She sat on the edge of the sofa now and placed her handbag next to her feet. Sam came to her side and hugged her. His once manly frame felt old and frail. Even his spine curved a little now as age had finally caught up with him. "She'll be over the moon that you've come. Is Teresa coming too?"

"Yes, but she will probably come later today or tomorrow. You know what she's like with her busy schedule, always rushing here and there."

"What about Jena, I thought you would have brought her along?"

"No Dad, I wanted the first time to be me and my mam. Jena will come soon, so stop worrying."

"I told your mam this morning you might come, and she's had me washing her hair and even putting a bit of slap on her. On my life, you would think the Queen was coming to see her. Fresh bedding on, and she's made me clean every inch of that bedroom too."

"I'm just going to have a few minutes and then I'll go in and see her."

He patted her shoulder and said softly, "I'm glad you are here. And it's probably for the best that our Shannon hasn't shown up again yet. I thought she would have been back by now. She said she was telling the women's refuge she was moving in here, but I've not heard a peep from her since. It's a lot to take in, I suppose, after all these years. She'll come back when she's ready. You know what Shannon's like, her way or the highway."

Emily nodded. "Yep, she's never been one for doing things by the book, has she?"

Sam went into the kitchen and Emily looked around the room. She smiled as she saw all the old photographs of her and her sisters on the wall. She stood up to have a closer look. She sniggered as she examined one of Teresa in her school uniform. Oh my God, she had bunny teeth, and that haircut looked like she had been dragged through a hedge. And here was one of her. There she was, Miss Prim and Proper, nothing out of place. Even her bobbed haircut was on point. She must have been around fourteen years old in this picture. Not long before her mam left and it all fell apart. She stroked her finger along the photograph and paused when she spotted the captain's badge on her sweatshirt. Yes, she was the top girl in her class, the form captain, the one everyone looked up to. Teresa had always said she was a geek, and she only got the badge because she was a creep, a suck-up to the teacher, and she was probably right. She was a bookworm back then, always had her homework in on time and she never missed a day of school. Teresa was the opposite and so was Shannon. They both bunked school whenever they could, and they were not as academic as she was. Every time she tried to help them with homework, they carted her and told her to get a life. Teresa was boy-mad growing up. She always had a string of boys asking to take her out. Rumour had it she let boys have a grope in exchange for fags or money. Nothing had changed there then, had it? Emily never even kissed a boy until she was sixteen, and that was all Teresa's work. She'd made her go on a double date with her and some guy and his mate, and told her straight that she had to have a go at kissing somebody.

Teresa had been the first one of them to have sex too, and Shannon wasn't far behind her. Emily always told them she was waiting until she got married before she had sex. But there again, it was Teresa who took her on a night out, got her pissed and she ended up losing her virginity to a lad she didn't really know. It was not a night she was proud of and, even today, she blamed her sister for letting her get in such a state that she slept with a guy.

Emily sat back down as Sam walked in holding two cups of hot tea. She took one from him and had a quick sip. He had made it how he used to when she was younger, sweet and milky. "I've been looking at those photographs, Dad. Bloody hell, we look a state, all three of us. I can't believe you have not taken them down."

"I've got boxes of photographs of you all growing up. It's where we all look the happiest. I often sit looking at them when your mam is sleeping. The good old days, eh? I wish I could turn back the clock."

Emily had another mouthful of her tea and stood up. "I can't put it off any longer. I'm going to see my mam."

Sam walked into the bedroom first and Emily wasn't far behind him. Her breath caught in her throat – she'd thought of her mother as some kind of scarlet woman all these years, and now she looked like a little old lady, as frail as a bird.

Sam squeezed his wife's hand and smiled. "You have a visitor, Bren."

Brenda sat up in her bed and gestured her husband out of the way. "Come here, love, come here and give me a hug. Bloody hell, I never thought I would see you again. Come here while I kiss you."

Emily took a few seconds to steady herself.

Sam stood back and looked on. His wife had promised him she would go nowhere until she had seen her children again, but there was only one child left to see. Would she leave this world then, give up her fight? He looked at Emily, curled up with her mother as if the years lost meant nothing. He left the room quietly. This was their time now, time to speak the truth, time to forgive.

Emily lifted her head and saw her mother's face properly for the first time. Her eyes were still the same, maybe smaller, sunken, but they were the same eyes she remembered. Brenda looked ill, a grey cast on her skin, sunken cheek-bones, her chest rising faster and shallower than it should.

Emily sat up on the bed. "Mam, I'm so sorry. Dad told me his part in what happened all those years ago and, while I know you did something terrible after, I think I know now how you could have done it. I feel ashamed to say, but I'm not so different. You should have told us what he'd done to you, leaving you when I was a baby, we would have understood. It must have been so hard for you. How on Earth did you cope?"

Brenda's voice was barely more than a whisper. "It's the past, love. I forgave your dad and I blocked it out of mind. He was your dad and you needed him, so I held a lot of stuff in for years. I was broken at the time, but him coming back to me made me think I'd moved on. Until I got the chance for payback – then I did the same. I know two wrongs don't make a right, though – and it was you girls who had to bear it. But that's not all I need to ask forgiveness for."

Emily looked into her mother's eyes – she must mean about Shannon and Jena. She was on the verge of asking what she meant when she heard knocking on the front door. She couldn't hear who it was, but knew she'd have to hold her questions in. Brenda started coughing. Emily helped her sit up and rubbed her back. She picked up a glass of water, held it to her mam's mouth and helped her take a small sip, like she was helping a child. Sam was back now and he stood at the bedroom door with a concerned look.

"Emily, can I borrow you for a second, love?"

When she came out onto the landing, Sam's eyes were wide, and his voice low. "That was the police at the door. They were looking for Shannon. They said she's not been back to the refuge, and they are scared for her safety. I hope she's not gone back with that Paddy bloke; she promised me she would never go back to him, so I don't know where she could be."

Emily rolled her eyes. "Dad, we are talking about Shannon here. How many times has she been on the missing list over the years? She's probably gone to one of her so-called friends for a drink or something."

"No love, she swore down she was off the booze and the pills, and she was sorting herself out."

"Well, don't hold your breath. If she's up to her old tricks, I want nothing to do with her. And I don't want Jena anywhere near her."

Sam shook his head, stressed. "I know you always think I stick up for her, but she was telling the truth this time, I could see it in her eyes."

Emily had turned back to the bedroom when her phone started ringing, Archie's name flashed across the screen. She quickly answered the call. "Hiya, did you find her?" The colour drained from her cheeks as she sat on the top stair listening to Archie. "I'm coming now. Which hospital is she in?"

Emily ended the call and cried out. "Jena is in hospital, in a bad way, been beaten up." She ran to the front door.

Sam rushed behind her. "Ring me as soon as you've seen her and let me know she's alright, will you?"

"Yes, Dad, speak soon," she stuttered as she sprinted down the garden path.

As she gunned the car's ignition, she wondered who would do something like that to a defenceless teen. Then a thought crossed her mind. Was it John, acting on his threats? Emily wheel-spun the car from the pavement and sped off in the direction of North Manchester General. Nothing would stop her from getting to her little girl.

Chapter Twenty-Seven

Archie was by the doors of A&E as she arrived.

"Where is she? What have they said? Is she alright? Who did this to her?"

Archie pulled away and tried to calm her down. Everybody was looking at her. He guided her to a side corridor and sat her down. "The doctors are still with her, she's been attacked. She was found this morning in the early hours near the town centre."

Emily let out a scream like an injured animal. "I need to see her, make sure she's alright. Archie, if anything happens to her, I…" She dropped her head into her hands.

He sat by her side, comforting her. "Em, the doctors are with her and she's in good hands. She's conscious and hopefully she can shed some light on things. She'll tell the police everything, I'll make sure of it, and the bastards who have done this to her will be locked up behind bars. It's the best place for them, because, trust me, if I get my hands on them, I'll cut their balls off and make necklaces out of them."

The couple hugged each other tightly. Emily could hear Teresa's voice down the corridor. She'd told Archie to text her. She found a small room off the corridor and stepped inside. "Archie, bring Teresa in here."

He walked down the corridor to Teresa and beckoned his sister-in-law into the room. He sat her down and told her what had happened, expecting a flurry of questions.

Instead, she shot a look over at her sister. "I might know what this is about."

"What do you mean?" Archie said, while Emily was rooted to the spot, terrified her sister had picked this moment to reveal all.

Teresa cringed. "Right, don't start going ballistic, but Jena told me she owed money to some main heads."

"What the hell for?" Emily asked.

And here it was, the truth she'd been keeping from her sister. "I was sworn to secrecy. She begged me not to tell a soul, told me she would sort it out."

Emily snapped, "Sort what out? Teresa, just fucking tell me. My daughter is lying in a hospital bed in there and I need to know everything so I can tell the police."

Teresa hated that she had to break the code of silence. "She got herself in deeper than she could manage. She was selling sniff, got herself a habit while selling it too. She promised me she was going to stop but I guess the drugs got hold of her and she couldn't get out of it. I think she was paying the loan back in kind – you know..."

Emily jumped up from her seat as if boiling water had been poured all over her. "What the hell do you mean? Say it again, and this time slower so I can digest it. On my life this is a sick joke."

"Emily, sit back down, will you? I was helping her and told her if she ever touched that shit again, I would come straight to you and tell you everything. It must have been the guys she owed money to who got to her first."

Emily rushed from the room. Archie was clearly in shock. Teresa looked over at him and tried to offer some words of comfort. "As long as she is alright, we can sort everything else out."

Archie went bright red and spoke through clenched teeth. "I bet it was you who got her on the game. Yeah, you would have sorted that out for her."

"Give me a bit of credit, Archie. This is her own doing, fuck all to do with me – I was the one trying to get her clean."

"So, she just woke up one day and thought, I'll be an escort? Where on Earth did that come from, if not you?"

"Girls do it all the time – young women with no other avenue to take. So, take your blame elsewhere, mate. Now go and see if your wife is alright. This isn't about you."

Archie rushed out of the door and slammed it behind him. After a few minutes, he brought Emily back and sat her down.

"Sorry about before Teresa. I was angry and should never have spoken to you like that. Fuck me, this is unreal, my worst nightmare."

Teresa gave him a half-hearted smile and looked over at Emily. "We can sort all this out, sis. I've got back-up now. I'll make sure they go and see the wankers who did this to her. Each of them will be dealt with."

Emily's nostrils flared. "I want them sorted. I want them to feel pain like my daughter has. I don't care if she owed them money, they should never have done this to her."

The door opened and a doctor walked in. Archie was straight to his side; he'd met him an hour or so before when his daughter was admitted.

"Doctor, is she alright?" His voice was desperate, and he was hanging on his every word.

"Jena has some serious injuries, but she is going to be alright. The police are with her now, so as soon as they have finished speaking to her, you will be able to go and see her. She needs rest so please try not to stay too long with her."

Emily burst out crying and sat with her arms cradled around her body, rocking to and fro. Teresa ran to her side and hugged her. "Everything is going to be alright, sis, trust me, everything is going to be alright."

The doctor left and the three of them sat in silence, digesting what had been said today in this room.

Emily finally said, "I went to see Mam earlier."

Teresa nodded. "And?"

"She was happy to see me. We said a few things that had long needed saying. But I got the sense there's something she's holding back. She was about to say something when the police came round. Shannon is on the missing list. She never returned to the women's refuge after she went to visit my mam and they are worried about her."

"She'll be back with her fella. I'd bet my last quid she's back in his bed. She never learns."

Emily said, "That was my first thought but Dad seems to think not, said she was adamant she would never go back there after the way he'd been treating her. He'd been battering her, locking her away, she'd told my dad. Anyway, the police will have checked the address they had on file. I bet by the time we're out of here we'll know the score. But I swear, if she's shacked up with him again, I'll tell Dad. I've already said I don't want her anywhere near Jena if she's not straightened out."

Archie spoke without thinking. "It looks like Jena's got herself in trouble even without Shannon. Everyone makes mistakes. We can't all be perfect."

Emily opened her mouth to say something, but her own guilt closed it firmly shut. Teresa shared a similar look.

Archie looked at his wife and then Teresa – something was going down here for sure, something more than he knew about. "Come on, let's go and see if the police have finished talking to Jena. There is no point in getting angry with her. What's done is done and all we can do is support her through this bad time. We will get her all the helps she needs and help fix her. Like I said, we all make mistakes."

Emily knew now that was truer than her husband would ever know. The only problem was, some mistakes were deadly.

Chapter Twenty-Eight

Teresa was like a woman on a mission as she left the hospital, driving like a maniac, swerving in and out of the traffic. A couple of quick calls to the right people and she had the details of the men who had done Jena in. Once she'd given the names to Gavin it would be job done. There'd be no danger left to Emily or Jena. He was driving over to Manchester to meet her. Now she only had to work out what Shannon was playing at.

Teresa pulled up on the street where her youngest sister lived. Gavin was on his way to meet her, and she sat parked up in the side street facing her sister's house, watching it, looking for any signs of movement. The property had only one light on upstairs, dimly lit. She never took her eyes from the window in the hope she would spot Shannon, but she never did. Teresa sparked up a cigarette and opened the car window slightly. She sat up straight – there was movement from the house, someone was coming out. The guy was built like a shit-house door and, by the looks of him, he could handle himself. Was this Paddy? She dipped her head as she watched him lock the front door, then constantly look back over his shoulder as he walked down the garden path. Why would he go out and leave the light on upstairs? And the way he kept glancing back sat uneasily with her.

She flicked her cigarette butt from the window and gripped the steering wheel tightly, watching him like a hawk as he headed off in the opposite direction. She knew time wasn't on her side. She quickly pulled her mobile phone from her pocket and rang Gavin. "Where are you? The guy my little sister's meant to be with has just gone out. We need to be quick before he comes back. How long are you going to be?" Her face creased as he answered her. "Fucking hell, Gav, twenty minutes? He could be back by then if he's just nipped to the shop. I'm going in. Hurry up." She ended the call and shoved her mobile phone back in her pocket. The car door swung open, and her hair swept back from her face. She zipped her black bomber jacket up and stood for a few seconds thinking. It was do or die time.

She tried knocking on the door again and then she lifted the letterbox flap and shouted, "Shan, it's me, Teresa. Open the door, love."

No response. Teresa looked around the garden and found a pebble. Standing back, she aimed it at the top window. She was already searching for something else to fire up at the glass when she finally saw her sister's face at the window. She looked terrible – a swollen eye distorted her face and bruises were blooming over her pale skin. She was speaking but Teresa couldn't hear a word she was saying. Why wouldn't she open the damn thing?

Teresa cupped her hands around her mouth and shouted up to her, "Open the door."

Shannon was frantic behind the glass, shaking her head and Teresa knew something was wrong, very wrong indeed. She looked at the white PVC front door and bit her bottom lip. Could she take it down? There was no time to think, she had to give it a go. With all her might she ran, and shoulder-charged the door. It was a good try, but the door never budged, she wasn't strong enough. That Paddy guy had taken no chances. Looking around the garden again, she found a metal scaffolding bar and picked it up from the thick black mud. She could try ramming it at the door or she could go through the window. She yanked her sleeves over her hands and ran at the kitchen window with the steel bar. She attacked it like her life depended on it. It gave way in a shower of sharp fragments.

Once all the glass was smashed out, she gripped the window frame and yanked herself up through the gap. It wasn't the first time she'd smashed her way into somewhere, but she'd been a lot younger the last time she'd tried this. But she was inside. She looked down. She must have caught her leg on the glass. The blood was pumping out.

"Shannon," she screamed. "Shannon, where the hell are you?" She was living on borrowed time. If Paddy came back and saw his window smashed, it would be over. Teresa heard a muffled shout from upstairs. She gripped the banister and, despite the wound to her leg, she pulled herself up. Again, she shouted for her sister.

"Teresa, I'm in here, help me, please."

She ran to a locked door and, forgetting the pain she was in, booted it with all her might. The door swung open, and she saw her sister properly for the first time in years. She was like a ghost standing there before her.

Shannon gripped her big sister and pleaded with her. "He'll be back soon, please don't let him keep me here. Hurry up, we need to go."

Teresa looked down at her leg and winced. Blood was spreading like wildfire over her jeans. "Sure, but we need to get through the window. Mind yourself."

They ran down the stairs and Teresa pushed Shannon up first, her hands shaking. Shannon pulled herself carefully through the window and urged her sister to follow her. She could see Teresa was in pain. Once she'd got one leg out of the window, she struggled to pull her injured leg through.

But it was too late. Paddy was back. As he turned onto the path he let out a roar. First he dragged Shannon by the hair towards her sister, then pulled Teresa through the shattered frame.

"Who the fuck are you? How dare you come to my house, destroying my property?"

Teresa was clawing out at him, and he had to use two hands to hold her down. In an instant, Shannon broke free and stood shaking like a leaf behind him. He had his hands around Teresa's neck now and Shannon knew he'd not let go. The sight of him choking the life out of her sister was enough to snap her out of her shock. She reached down.

Paddy fell to the floor as the steel bar smashed over his head, once, twice, three times. Even when he went down, Shannon still swung the bar at his head.

Teresa rolled onto her side and scrambled to the other side of the garden. She could see her sister now stood over Paddy with the cold metal bar still held firmly in her hands.

"Shannon," she yelped. "Come on, we need to go." Teresa knew if she left her a second longer, her sister would end him once and for all. "He's not worth the charge sheet, love. Leave him to rot. Come on, let's get you out of here."

The two of them stumbled out of the garden and headed straight to the car. Once inside, Teresa flicked the engine over and screeched out onto the street. She rummaged in her pocket and found her mobile phone. Her hands were shaking vigorously, and she could hardly speak. "Gav, I've got her. Head back home. The fucker's been done in. He's flat out in the garden. Don't go near the house because the dibble will be there soon. I've fucked my leg up too, gushing in blood, it is. Lucky I'm headed back to the hospital."

Teresa stayed on the phone for a few minutes more before she ended the call. Her eyes stayed on the road, and she was breathing heavily. "Do me a favour, Shannon, find something to tie around my leg to stop the bleeding. Tie it tight or else I won't be able to stay conscious, let alone drive."

Shannon yanked her jumper off and took off the t-shirt she was wearing underneath it. She lifted Teresa's leg up and shoved the t-shirt underneath it before dragging at the fabric and tying it up as tight as she could.

Teresa screamed out in pain.

"I can't stop the bleeding, Teresa. Honest on my life, the blood is still pumping out of it."

"Fuck me, Shannon, that man is a nutter. How long has he had you locked up in there?"

"He tracked me down outside Mam and Dad's house. I should have known he'd find me."

"Well, he won't come after you anymore. He'll be lucky if he walks at all after the hiding you just gave him. I'll drop you at Dad's, and then I'll go and get sorted out. I've not been to see Mam yet but please tell her I'll come as soon as I'm patched up." Teresa was gasping as she stopped at the lights. "And you may as well know – it's not just me. Jena has been attacked, Shan. She's in a bad way in the hossy, but she's going to be OK. Emily and Archie are there with her and the doctor said she's lucky to be alive."

Shannon looked sick. "What the fuck? Who would do something like that to her? I need to go and see her, make sure she is alright. You said when you sided with Emily and Dad that we were giving my baby girl a better life with Emily and Archie. And now look what's happened."

"Stay put. I've told you she's going to be alright; she's got herself mixed up in some shit and, now everyone knows about it, she should be alright."

"Shit like what? Don't tell me half the story, I want to know everything. She is my daughter, after all. I know you all don't think I care about her, but I do. Every day I think about her. She's constantly on my mind. I'm sick of the lies. Jena is my daughter and, just because I messed up, it's like I have to pay for the rest of my life. I'm a woman now, not a kid, and you can't all speak to me like I don't know my own mind. I've had a lot of time to think lately and it's probably the first time in ages that I've had a straight head. I want my girl, my baby, to know the truth."

Teresa banged her hand on the steering wheel. "Don't start causing any more shit in this family right now. Mam's on her deathbed, Emily has been going through shit, and I was on the brink of doing a runner. We've all been through enough, and it would tip us over the edge if you told Jena the truth right now. Emily took her on and has looked after that kid since she's been born. It would break her heart if you told Jena the truth."

"It's always been about everyone else, Teresa. What about me for a change? What about how I feel? Because, let me tell you, I've felt empty for years."

Teresa stopped the car outside her parents' house and reached across to touch her sister's hand. "I'm not saying never, I'm just saying not yet. Look at the three of us – Emily's at the hossy having a panic attack, you look like you've been ten rounds with Tyson, and I've got a slash to my leg that Jack the Ripper would be proud of. Let's get patched up, make sure Jena is back on her feet, and then you, me and Emily can sit down and have the conversation. We've waited years – another few days ain't going to kill us."

Shannon wiped her tears away with her sleeve. "As long as we do. We can't brush this under the carpet like we do everything else. We have to deal with it and make it right. I don't want to be like Mam – keeping secrets til my dying breath."

Teresa nodded slowly and swallowed hard. "Go inside. Get a warm bath and a hot drink. Tell Dad Paddy caught up with you but it's over now – tell him the dibble have come for him – but I'd not tell him about your trick with the scaffolding bar. There are some things he doesn't need to know. Not now, not ever."

Shannon opened the car door and turned back before she left. "OK. Now please go and get your leg sorted. And tell Jena... tell Jena Auntie Shannon will see her soon."

John Spencer was watching the television with a spliff hanging from his mouth when his front door caved in. He didn't even have time to stand up. Gavin was straight on him, making sure this time he had the upper hand. He was team-handed, and his boys pinned John down.

"Hello, my old friend. I bet you never thought you would see me again, did you? Unlucky bastard, aren't you? I know everyone around here and it was just a matter of time before I caught up with you. Not so cocky when you're not carrying, are you?"

John knew the outcome of this attack before it started. He saw the gun in Gavin's hand and, although he tried to break free, he never stood a chance.

The gun fired and John's legs shook for a few seconds before he was motionless. The men holding him down let his body drop to the sofa like a lead weight. None of them held one bit of remorse for what they had done. It was all in a day's work.

Gavin blew his warm breath over the end of the gun. "Fucking cover him up and dump the bastard in the canal. Tie some bricks to him so he goes straight to the bottom with all the other shit."

Chapter Twenty-Nine

Teresa sat in her car outside her parents' house and looked down at her injured leg. She'd had eight stitches, and the doctors told her how lucky she was because the glass had just missed a main artery. She just hoped there wasn't a police report out about a blood-stained broken window next to the site of an attempted murder. She was sailing close to the wind – even for her.

She was sat scrolling the news headlines. All she had told Emily was that John would never bother her again and, when her sister saw the report on the local news, she would know not to ask any more questions. The police had raided his house and found no suspects but had made a haul of guns linking him to several armed robberies in the area. Teresa kept an eye on the news, but she knew the police wouldn't be looking too hard for John. Rough justice.

Jena was out of hospital now and, after hours of crying when she came clean to Emily and Archie, she was on the mend – with a promise to herself and her parents that she'd clean up her act. Archie wanted her to go to rehab, but she told them straight that, now all this worry and stress was off her head, she could get back on track without any help. She had even started talking about college qualifications.

Jena was meant to be here too; the whole family back together as one at last. But she didn't know if she could face it. Teresa had built her life on never looking back. Just then a text alert pinged on Teresa's phone, a number she hadn't thought she'd see again.

> Hi babes, I've missed you, missed our hotel dates. There is only you who makes me feel good. Time to start working off that loan. I need to see you again. Meet me at our special place tonight at eight o'clock? Teddy xxx

Teresa read through the message again and again. Well, this was a turn up for the books. She deleted the message instantly and placed her phone back on the side. Her mind was doing overtime; she had some big decisions to make now. She could live her life with Gavin and be at his beck and call until he got fed up of her, or she could be Teddy's mistress. Or maybe, just maybe, it was time to go it alone. She had her sisters now, after all.Teresa knew coming back to her parents' house after all these years was not going to be easy. Shannon and Emily had already made their peace with Mam, and all eyes would be on her from the moment she stepped inside the house.

She would be judged for the life she chose, for the son she gave up. They wouldn't say she was a bad mother, but the way they would look at her would tell all she needed to know.

She sat parked up outside the house, staring at it. Behind that door was her past. She could see silhouettes of her family members behind the drawn curtains. No doubt they were all talking about days gone by, the laughter they all shared, looking at old photos. She would recognise the girl she used to be in pictures, but she was different now, not that same innocent who left her home so many years ago. She had loved her mother more than words could say once, but she had mourned her the day she left. Did she really need to say goodbye all over again? She had a vision of her mother still in her mind, and seeing her now, ill, at death's door, would spoil that. Her mum had two of her daughters back by her side. That was better than none, wasn't it? Teresa turned the key in the ignition and pulled off onto the road.

Emily kept looking at her wristwatch and checking the time. She whispered to Archie, "Where the hell is she? She said she would be here by now. I bet she's not even ready yet, you know what she's like, I bet she's getting dressed to the nines for her big entrance. She always liked to be the centre of attention, didn't she?"

"She sure did. Relax and have another drink."

Emily touched his fingers softly. "I know I have not been the best wife lately, but as from today me and you are going to be happy. I'm sick of arguing and being miserable. I don't know about you, but I want to start again and put the past behind us. Seeing my mam and dad together has made me realise that life is too short to be angry all the time. I want us to travel together, go and see the world, have fun again like we did in the old days. I'd been putting money aside for a new car – but let's use it to go somewhere nice. I could do with a change of scene after all this – we both could."

Archie choked up. This conversation had been a long time coming. "I love you more now than I ever have. You're right, this is our time now and I'm so glad you have settled things with your mam. I knew it was always at the back of your mind. Come here and give me a kiss. I love you, Em. I love you all the world and back again."

Emily kissed her husband and her tears stuck to his cheek. They held each other tightly and they looked like they were never letting go. Jena clocked them and cringed. She headed to the kitchen to get a drink.

Shannon stood up too and smiled softly.

Jena said, "Do you want a wine, Shan? Those two love-birds are doing my head in, all over each other. They're knocking me sick. There should be a law against old people kissing in public, shouldn't there?" she chuckled.

Shannon put her arm around Jena's waist. "I'm not drinking anymore, love. I'll have a glass of orange. I've promised my mam I won't touch another drop, and I can't go breaking promises, can I?"

Jena sat down on the kitchen chair and poured two glasses of orange. "You and me both, Shan. I've messed up so much lately and I want to get my life back on track. I'm more like you than anyone, aren't I? Two peas in a pod."

Shannon shot a look through the doorway. Archie and Emily were still cuddled together. She nodded. "We are alike, Jena. Like you said, two peas in a pod. The only difference is I'm too old to make a fresh start now, I've got some scars that won't ever go – but you've got everything ahead of you. Go out there and prove them all wrong. Show all those haters you can be successful, then come back to Manchester with a spring in your step. You can be anything you want to be, if you have self-belief. I'm going to get a job too. I'm thinking about working at the refuge a few days a week helping women who have been through the same as me. They said they always need volunteers with real life experience. Every cloud and all that."

"That's amazing, Shan. For the record, you have always been my favourite auntie, the only one who always sent me a card on my birthday and at Christmas time. Even when we hadn't seen you for years, you never forgot the day. That meant a lot to me, showed you cared, you never forgot about me."

Shannon held back the tears and hugged Jena. She pulled away and looked her straight in the eyes. "Go and make me proud. Be the best version of yourself that you can be. I love you, Jena, and I'm always here for you, only ever a phone call away."

Jena nodded. What Shannon said to her made sense. Getting out of Manchester might be the fresh start she needed.

They were gathered in Brenda's bedroom. Sam sat with her on the bed, talking away, laughing and joking. But when he got up to go and get a drink, Archie and Jena took the hint and left the sisters alone with their mother. The elderly woman reached out and clasped their hands.

"I know we're missing Teresa. My middle girl, my rule-breaker. But I can't wait any longer to share this, sweethearts."

Shannon wanted her mam to rest easy. "It's OK. You've told us everything we need to know. Now we know about Dad's affair, it makes more sense of what you did. I'm not saying it was right but, like Emily, I've crossed lines myself. We're all human."

"No love, there's more. You all wondered why your dad and I stuck it out? I need you to know. Sometimes it's love that binds you – sometimes it's evil." Brenda paused.

"What do you mean, Mam? You've got to forgive yourself for the affair. Dad did, after all. It was wrong, yes, but not evil." Emily felt these words were as much to comfort herself as her mother.

"No, pet. It's not the affair I'm talking about – it's what happened after. Did you ever wonder why I came back? You girls were grown and gone. Shannon, you'd had a baby of your own by the time I realised how stupid I'd been. Shagging your dad's best mate seemed like revenge. But it soon turned sour for me. He was a monster. It wasn't only your dad he leathered. I thought it was what I deserved for what I'd done. Until one day your dad saw me out in town – bruised and battered. His scars had healed but he knew immediately where I'd got mine."

Shannon shuddered. Her mam had been through what she'd suffered at Paddy's hands.

"He told me we needed revenge. But what copper would believe me? It was all ignored back then, just another domestic. So we decided to take things into our own hands."

Emily was horror-struck.

"Haven't you wondered why he let me go back to your dad? Where he's been all these years?" Brenda shut her eyes.

"Mam, what do you mean?" Shannon pressed.

"We settled the score. He's in the bottom of the canal, Ancoats way. There, I've said it. It's the truth at last. Your dad and me – we hurt each other. But in the end, we'd kill for each other."

Emily swallowed. Maybe the apple didn't fall too far from the tree after all. What was she meant to do with this knowledge?

"Mam, it must be your pills making you say stuff. At least that's what I'll tell Dad if he ever asks anything. It may be the truth, but it's also the past. It's clean slate time – for all of us. We need to let it go. We need to let you go. You're free now, Mam." Emily blinked away her tears as the others bundled back into the room.

Tonight Brenda had more life and sparkle than she had done in weeks. Emily and Archie sat by the bedside with Shannon and Jena clustered at the other end. Nobody realised she had slipped away until it was too late. Brenda had a beautiful smile on her face and looked at peace. Sam smiled too as he looked at his wife. She had been a fighter until the end and never gave up believing her girls would come back home. Two out of three wasn't bad, he figured. You never got everything you wanted in life. Teresa would make her own peace with her mam's passing, he knew that. There were tears in the bedroom as they each said goodbye to Brenda in their own way. She had been a woman of substance – surprising them right up to the last – and she would never be forgotten.

"Rest in peace," murmured Sam as, at last, he sat alone in the twilight with her.

Epilogue

Not so far away, in a different part of town, Teresa sat waiting for Teddy in the luxurious hotel he had booked. This woman looked on point tonight: patent high-heeled shoes, tight-fitted black dress. She smelt gorgeous too and, apart from the bandage on her leg, she looked like a magazine model. She looked out of the window onto Manchester town centre and smiled. There were so many lights and buildings staring straight back at her. This was her home town and where her heart was. She would be sad to leave it to move to another country, but her time here was done. Too many bad memories. She wanted a new beginning, a new life where nobody knew her name. Tonight was her farewell tour. One last trick before she went. She owed Teddy that much.

The door opened and closed behind her. She still gazed on the cityscape as she said softly, "I'm glad you had a re-think, Teddy. I told you time and time again I would be your mistress. I can give you everything you need – and I mean everything. We can have a good life, me and you, and the good thing is it's not going to cost you an extra penny."

There was no reply. Teresa turned slowly and flicked her hair over her shoulder, smiling from cheek to cheek, ready to show Teddy what he'd been missing.

Her jaw dropped when she saw an older woman stood facing her. Smart, timid – not the kind of person she would expect to see in a place like this. "I think you have the wrong room, my dear. This is my room."

The older woman stood firm, shoulders back, and sneered at her. "Do you think I never knew about you with my husband? I bet he told you I didn't understand him and he was only with me because of our children, didn't he?"

Puzzled, Teresa edged forward. "Listen, I don't know who you are, but you have the wrong person and the wrong room. Can you leave, please?"

The woman's hand was shaking as she dug deep into her long coat. She pulled out a silver pistol and pointed it at Teresa. "I know about all the meetings you had with my Ted, all those dirty nights you two shared together, and I also know he paid you off. I do his accounts. Of course I was going to see through his stories of investments and loans. How did he think I would not find out? It beats me. I've known for a very long time, lovey. The dirty bastard has been seeing prostitutes for as long as I can remember. You're one of many, nothing special. But I looked the other way until you got your claws into my money. Did you think you could walk away with my cash, and I wouldn't bat an eye? Think again, you hussy."

Teresa was as white as a ghost. Slowly she stepped forward.

"One more step and I'll pull the trigger. I want my money back, every last penny of it."

Teresa smirked. Who on Earth did this old girl think she was talking to? She would eat her alive. As if she'd have the balls to pull the trigger.

Teresa took a swift step forward and went to take the gun from Teddy's wife's hand.

Before she knew what had happened, there was a bang and a feeling like heat and cold all at once ran through her. She was on the floor.

As the other woman let herself out softly, Teresa lay motionless, sightless eyes staring at the ceiling. She wasn't leaving Manchester after all.

Acknowledgements

Thank you to James for his support.
My children: Ashley, Blake, Declan, Darcy and
all my grandchildren.
Thanks to Gen, Megan, and Alice as well as
all the crew at HarperNorth.
Finally, thank you to all my readers and followers.

Book Credits

HarperNorth would like to thank the following staff and contributors for their involvement in making this book a reality:

Fionnuala Barrett
Samuel Birkett
Peter Borcsok
Ciara Briggs
Sarah Burke
Alan Cracknell
Jonathan de Peyer
Anna Derkacz
Morgan Dun-Campbell
Tom Dunstan
Kate Elton
Sarah Emsley
Simon Gerratt
Monica Green
Natassa Hadjinicolaou
CJ Harter
Megan Jones
Jean-Marie Kelly
Taslima Khatun
Sammy Luton
Rachel McCarron
Molly McNevin
Benjamin McConnell
Petra Moll
Alice Murphy-Pyle
Adam Murray
Genevieve Pegg
Agnes Rigou
Florence Shepherd
Eleanor Slater
Emma Sullivan
Katrina Troy
Daisy Watt
Sarah Whittaker